Mary Maxwell-Scott

Abbotsford

the personal relics and antiquarian treasures of Sir Walter Scott -

Illustrated by William Gibb

Mary Maxwell-Scott

Abbotsford

the personal relics and antiquarian treasures of Sir Walter Scott - Illustrated by William Gibb

ISBN/EAN: 9783337387198

Printed in Europe, USA, Canada, Australia, Japan

Cover: Foto ©Andreas Hilbeck / pixelio.de

More available books at **www.hansebooks.com**

ABBOTSFORD

THE

PERSONAL RELICS AND ANTIQUARIAN TREASURES

OF

SIR WALTER SCOTT

DESCRIBED BY

THE HON. MARY MONICA MAXWELL SCOTT

OF ABBOTSFORD

AND

ILLUSTRATED BY WILLIAM GIBB

LONDON
ADAM AND CHARLES BLACK
, 1893

STONE CARVINGS FROM GARDEN SCREEN

CONTENTS

ORNAMENTAL CHAPTER HEADINGS

ARCHBISHOP SHARP'S GRATE, AND ROMAN POT. | CARVED PANELS FROM ERSKINE'S PULPIT.
BACK OF CHAIR AT ABBOTSFORD. | PANELS FROM "SPEAK A BIT."
                STONE CARVINGS FROM GARDEN SCREEN.

INTRODUCTION

THE drawing of Abbotsford House has been fitly chosen as the frontis-piece to this series of illustrations of Sir Walter's treasures, so beautifully drawn by Mr. Gibb; I have therefore endeavoured to gather together the chief facts relating to the building, so as to give a short connected account of the "Making of Abbotsford."[1] No words of mine are needed to remind my readers of Sir Walter's love for his home. We know that, as in joy, so also in sorrow and loss, and to the very end, his thoughts turned constantly to Abbotsford. As Mr. Lockhart truly says, "to have curtailed the exposition of his fond untiring enthusiasm on that score, would have been like omitting the Prince in a cast of Hamlet." It was in his early youth that Sir Walter first saw the site of the future Abbotsford. "I have often heard him tell," writes Mr. Lockhart, "that when travelling in his boyhood with his father, from Selkirk to Melrose, the old man suddenly desired the carriage to halt at the foot of an eminence, and said, 'We must get out here, Walter, and see a thing quite in your line.' His father then conducted him to a

[1] The following pages relate to Sir Walter's Abbotsford only; but I may be permitted to add that the wing to the west of the square tower and the new south front were built by my father and completed in 1858. To him also we owe the present arrangement of terraces and of the courtyard garden.—M. M. M. S.

rude stone on the edge of an acclivity, about half a mile above the Tweed at Abbotsford, which marks the spot

> 'Where-gallant Cessford's life-blood dear
> Reeked on dark Elliott's border spear.'

This was the conclusion of the battle of Melrose, fought in 1526, between the Earls of Angus and Home and the two chiefs of the race of Kerr on the one side, and Buccleuch and his clan on the other, in sight of the young King James V., the possession of whose person was the object of the contest. The battle is often mentioned in the *Border Minstrelsy*. . . . In the names of various localities between Melrose and Abbotsford, such as *Skirmish-field*, *Charge-law*, and so forth, the incidents of the fight have found a lasting record; and the spot where the retainer of Buccleuch terminated the pursuit of the victors by the mortal wound of Kerr of Cessford (ancestor of the Dukes of Roxburghe) has always been called *Turn-again*." [1]

Sir Walter probably never forgot this incident, for when, in 1811, he determined to become a "Tweedside Laird," he fixed upon the little property which, though then "not a very attractive one to the general observer, had long been one of peculiar interest" to him.

On the 12th May 1811, Sir Walter writes to James Ballantyne upon business, and adds: "My attention has been a little dissipated by considering a plan for my own future comfort which I hasten to mention to you. My lease of Ashestiel is out . . . I have therefore resolved to purchase a piece of ground sufficient for a cottage and a few fields. There are two pieces, either of which would suit me, but both would make a very desirable property indeed. They stretch along the Tweed, near halfway between Melrose and Selkirk, on the opposite side from Lord Somerville, and could be had for between £7000 and £8000, or either separate for about half the sum. I have serious thoughts of one or both, and must have recourse to my pen to make the matter easy."

Of the two adjoining farms here mentioned, Sir Walter soon after bought the one comprising *Turn-again*. The person from whom he bought the property was a valued friend of his own, Dr. Robert Douglas, minister of Galashiels. He had never resided on the property, and the only embellishments he had effected had been "limited to one stripe of firs, so long and so narrow that Scott likened it to a black

---

[1] *Turn-again* is situated in the wood to the left above the house. *Life* (in 10 vols.), vol. iii. p. 335.

hair-comb. It ran from the precincts of the homestead towards *Turn-again*, and has bequeathed the name of *the Doctor's redding-kame* to the mass of nobler trees amidst which its dark straight line can now hardly be traced."[1]

Clarty Hole, as the farm was termed, seems to have deserved its inharmonious name; the haugh or meadow by the river with about a hundred acres of undulating ground at the back, were alike in a most neglected state, "undrained, wretchedly enclosed, much of it covered with nothing better than the native heath. The farm-house itself was small and poor, with a common *kail-yard* on one flank and a staring barn, of the doctor's erection, on the other." But, as Mr. Lockhart says, the Tweed was everything to Sir Walter, and from the moment he took possession, "he claimed for his farm the name of the adjoining *ford*, situated just above the influx of the classical tributary Gala. As might be guessed from the name of Abbotsford, all these lands had belonged of old to the great Abbey of Melrose."[2]

The neighbourhood of two antiquarian remains of interest lent an additional charm to the little property in Sir Walter's eyes. To the left of the site of the house we can still see the old Roman road leading down to the ford, while on the hill opposite Abbotsford may be traced the *Catrail* so often mentioned in Sir Walter's early letters to Mr. Ellis.

In a letter to his brother-in-law Mr. Carpenter, dated 5th August, Sir Walter describes his new property, adding, "I intend building a small cottage here for my summer abode, being obliged by law, as well as by inclination, to make this county my residence for some months every year. This is the greatest incident which has lately taken place in our domestic concerns. And I assure you we are not a little proud of being greeted as *laird* and *lady* of *Abbotsford*." And again, in a letter to Joanna Baillie, written the same week, the new Abbotsford is thus mentioned: "My schemes about my cottage go on; of about a hundred acres I have manfully resolved to plant from sixty to seventy; as to my scale of dwelling, why you shall see my plan when I have adjusted it. My present intention is to have only two spare bedrooms with dressing-rooms, each of which will, on a pinch, have a couch bed; but I cannot relinquish my border principle of accommodating all the cousins and *duniwastles* who will rather sleep in chairs and on the floor, and in the hay-loft, than be absent when folks are gathered together."

[1] *Life*, vol. iii. p. 339.   [2] *Ibid.* vol. iii. p. 340.

Sir Walter lost no time in planning his future residence, and begged Mr. Stark [1] to give him a design for an ornamental cottage in the style of the old English vicarage house.

But before his wishes could be met, Mr. Stark died, and his building plans, checked for a time, expanded by degrees; and in place of the cottage the present Abbotsford gradually took form. Sir Walter's first plans for his house are sketched in a letter to Mr. Morritt: "I have fixed only two points," he writes, "respecting my intended cottage; one is that it shall be *in* my garden, or rather kail-yard, the other that the little drawing-room shall open into a little conservatory, in which conservatory there shall be a fountain. These are articles of taste which I have long since determined upon, but I hope before a stone of my paradise is begun we shall meet and collogue upon it."

By the following year some little progress had been made, and such improvements as "a good garden wall and complete stables in the Haugh" are mentioned in a letter to Terry. In the spring of 1814 Sir Walter presses the Morritts to visit him. "I am arranging this cottage a little more conveniently," he writes, "to put off the plague and expense of building another year; and I assure you I expect to spare Mrs. Morritt and you a chamber in the wall, with a dressing-room and everything handsome about you. You will not stipulate of course for many square feet." In the autumn Sir Walter says, in a letter to Mr. Terry: "I wish you saw Abbotsford, which begins this season to look the whimsical, gay, odd cabin that we had chalked out. . . . I have made the old farmhouse my *corps de logis*, with some outlying places for kitchen, laundry, and two spare bedrooms which run along the east wall of the farm-court not without some picturesque effect." Two years later a letter to the same friend, dated November 1816, and written from Edinburgh, reports further progress; after mentioning the arrival of Mr. Bullock and Mr. Blore, to both of whom Abbotsford was to owe much, Sir Walter continues: "I have had the assistance of both these gentlemen in arranging an addition to the cottage at Abbotsford, intended to connect the present farmhouse with the line of low buildings to the right of it. Mr. Bullock will show you the plan, which I think is very ingenious. He has promised to give it his consideration with respect to the interior; and Mr. Blore has drawn me a very handsome elevation both to the road and to the river. . . . This addition will give me first a handsome boudoir. . . .

[1] An Edinburgh architect of whose talents Sir Walter had a high opinion.

This opens into the little drawing-room to which it serves as a chapel of ease; and on the other side to a handsome dining parlour of 27 feet by 18, with three windows to the north, and one to the south, the last to be Gothic and filled with stained glass. Besides these commodities, there is a small conservatory or green-house, and a study for myself which we design to fit up with ornaments from Melrose Abbey. . . . Abbotsford is looking pretty at last, and the planting is making some show."

By the July of 1817 the foundations of that portion of Abbotsford which extends from the hall westwards to the square tower had apparently been laid, and in September Sir Walter writes to Joanna Baillie that the building is about to be roofed in, "and a comical concern it is," he adds.

The projected *tower* seems to have suggested some criticism from Mr. Terry, to which Sir Walter replies : " I agree with you that the tower will look rather rich for the rest of the building ; yet you may be assured that with diagonal chimneys and notched gables it will have a very fine effect, and is in Scotch architecture by no means incompatible." A few days later Sir Walter again writes to Mr. Terry detailing plans for the new house, of which he says : "Wilkie admires the whole as a composition, and that is high authority. . . . I do not believe I should save £100 by retaining *Mrs. Redford*[1] by the time she was raised, altered, and beautified ; for, like the Highlandman's gun, she wants stock, lock, and barrel, to put her into repair. In the meantime 'the cabin is convenient.'"

Some months later Sir Walter could congratulate himself on the strength of the new building. " I have reason to be proud," he writes, "of the finishing of my castle, for even of the tower, for which I trembled, not a stone has been shaken by the late terrific gale which blew a roof clear off in the neighbourhood."

It was in the autumn of this year, 1818, that Mr. Lockhart first saw Abbotsford, and he confesses that it then had a fantastic appearance, being but a fragment of the existing edifice, and not at all harmonising in its outline with " Mother Redford's original tenement to the eastward"; but he continues, "Scott, however, expatiated *con amore* on the rapidity with which, being chiefly of darkish granite, it was assuming a 'time-honoured' aspect." Later in the same evening Mr. Lockhart tells us how the younger portion of the party, headed by Sir Walter, ascended the *tower* and viewed the Tweed and Melrose by moonlight.[2]

---

[1] The original farmhouse.   [2] *Life*, vol. v. pp. 375, 376.

In the spring of 1820 Sir Walter writes to Lady Scott from London : "I have got a delightful plan for the addition at Abbotsford, which I think will make it quite complete, and furnish me with a handsome library, and you with a drawing-room and better bedroom, with good bedrooms for company, etc. It will cost me a little hard work to meet the expense, but I have been a good while idle." On his return from town, Sir Walter brought Mr. Blore's detailed plans for this, the completion of Abbotsford, including the wall and gateway of the courtyard to the south and the graceful arched and carved stone screen which divides the court from the gardens. The latter, however, had been originally devised by Sir Walter himself. "The foundations might have been set about without further delay ; but he was very reluctant to authorise the demolition of the rustic porch of the old cottage, with its luxuriant overgrowth of roses and jessamines ; and, in short, could not make up his mind to sign the death-warrant of this favourite bower until winter had robbed it of its beauties."[1] The building operations continued throughout the year, and in the summer of 1822 the house was, to use Sir Walter's expression, "like a cried fair," with the masons busy at work, and the numerous guests from the south, who, after engaging in the festivities of the royal visit in Edinburgh, hastened to Abbotsford.

In October Sir Walter writes to his son : "My new house is quite finished as to masonry, and we are now getting on the roof, just in time to face the bad weather." In the August of the following year Miss Edgeworth visited the almost completed Abbotsford, and her impressions are charmingly summed up in her greeting to Sir Walter, who received her at the archway to the courtyard. "Everything about you is exactly what one ought to have had wit enough to dream."

Thus by the beginning of 1825 Abbotsford was ready for the "house-warming," that joyous occasion so pleasantly described in the *Life.*[2] Who could then have foreseen that before the year was over heavy clouds of misfortune would hang over Abbotsford, and cause Sir Walter to write such words as these in his *Journal :* 18th December, "sad hearts at Darnick and in the cottages of Abbotsford . . . I have half resolved never to see the place again. How could I tread my hall with such a diminished crest ? How live a poor indebted man where I was once the wealthy—the honoured ?" And again, 22nd January 1826, "I have

---

[1] *Life*, vol. vi. p. 388.   [2] See vol. vii. pp. 293, etc., 344.

walked my last on the domains I have planted—sate the last time in the halls I have built. But death would have taken them from me if misfortune had spared them." [1]

Happily this foreboding was not fulfilled, and many tranquil days were still to be spent at Abbotsford. It may perhaps be of interest to insert here an extract from a description of the house as it appeared during this year. The account is taken from a magazine article published in 1829, written in the character of an imaginary American, supposed to visit Abbotsford during the summer of 1825, in Sir Walter's absence. [2]

After describing the changes wrought in the surroundings of Abbotsford by Sir Walter's patient plantings and judicious improvements, the writer continues: "But I am keeping you too long away from 'The Roof-tree of Monkbarns,' which is situated on the brink of the last of a series of irregular hills, descending from the elevation of the Eildons to the Tweed. On all sides, except towards the river, the house connects itself with the gardens (according to the old fashion now generally condemned);—so that there is no want of air and space about the habitation. The building is such a one, I daresay, as nobody but he would ever have dreamed of erecting; or, if he had, escaped being quizzed for his pains. Yet it is eminently imposing in its general effect; and in most of its details, not only full of historical interest, but beauty also. It is no doubt a thing of shreds and patches, but they have been combined by a masterly hand; and if there be some whimsicalities, that in an ordinary case might have called up a smile, who is likely now or hereafter to contemplate such a monument of such a man's peculiar tastes and fancies, without feelings of a far different order? By the principal approach you come very suddenly on the edifice;—as the French would say, 'Vous *tombez* sur le chateau'; but this evil, if evil it be, was unavoidable, in consequence of the vicinity of a public road, which cuts off the *chateau* and its *plaisance* from the main body of park and wood. The gateway is a lofty arch rising out of an embattled wall of considerable height; and the *jougs*, as they are styled, those well-known emblems of feudal authority, hang rusty at the side; this pair being relics from that great citadel of the old Douglasses, Thrieve Castle in Galloway. On entering, you

---

[1] *Journal*, vol. i. pp. 52, 89.

[2] The paper on Abbotsford from which I give this extract was published as a keepsake, called the "Anniversary," and added by Mr. Lockhart to the second edition of the *Life* (in 10 vols.), vol. vii. p. 395.

find yourself within an enclosure of perhaps half an acre, two sides thereof being protected by the high wall above mentioned, all along which, inside, a trellised walk extends itself—broad, cool, and dark overhead with roses and honeysuckles. The third side, to the east, shows a screen of open arches of Gothic stone-work, filled between with a net-work of iron, not visible until you come close to it, and affording therefore delightful glimpses of the gardens, which spread upwards with many architectural ornaments of turret, porch, urn, vase, etc. This elegant screen abuts on the eastern extremity of the house, which runs along the whole of the northern side (and a small part of the western) of the great enclosure. . . . The house is more than 150 feet long in front, as I paced it; was built at two different onsets; has a tall tower at either end, the one not the least like the other; presents sundry *crowfooted, alias zigzagged,* gables to the eye : a myriad of indentations and parapets, and machicolated eaves; most fantastic waterspouts; labelled windows, not a few of them painted glass; groups of right Elizabethan chimneys; balconies of diverse fashions, greater and lesser; stones carved with heraldries innumerable, let in here and there in the wall, and a very noble projecting gateway—a facsimile, I am told, of that appertaining to a certain dilapidated royal palace." [1]

The story of the building of Abbotsford now ends. A few more years and we come to the very affecting account, given by Mr. Lockhart, of Sir Walter's last return to his home. Let me conclude with his own words : " I have seen much," he kept saying, " but nothing like my ain house." [2]

In the notes which follow I have attempted to give some history of Sir Walter's " gabions"; but the graceful drawings which head the letterpress, as well as the drawings of the Roman pot and ancient grate, require some separate notice. The Roman pot is so admirably described in the *Reliquiæ Trottcosianæ* [3] that we cannot do better than quote the passage : " On the hearth before the grate is placed a bronze pot of the largest size, which was found about twenty years since in the domain of Riddle, in Roxburghshire. It happened that the housemaid, with unnecessary prodigality of domestic labour, had bestowed on the bronze pot several coatings of black-lead when she was burnishing the utensils of the kitchen with that substance.

---

[1] Linlithgow. [2] *Life*, vol. x. p. 209.

[3] " The descriptive Catalogue of that collection " (the Abbotsford Museum) " which he began towards the close of his life, but, alas ! never finished, is entitled *Reliquiæ Trottcosianæ—or the Gabions of the late Jonathan Oldbuck, Esq.*" *Life*, vol. v. p. 143.

It chanced, at a sale of household goods by auction, that the present proprietor and a gentleman of rank in the neighbourhood were contending with emulation for the possession of what they well knew, especially from its size, was a gabion of great merit. This produced no little amazement among the uninitiated, of whom there were a considerable number present, when an old woman, after a long look at the countenance first of one bidder and then of the other, at length ejaculated with a sigh, when the contest was over: 'Heigh, sirs, the foundry wark must be sair up in Edinburgh, to see the great folk bidding that gait about a kale pot!' 'Aweel,' she added, in a tone of submission, 'it's needless for me to wait for the frying-pan if the kale pot is gaun to gae for a' thae guineas,' with which declaration the good lady left the auction." The same authority instructs us regarding Archbishop Sharp's grate: "The chimney grate inserted under this ancient arch was the property of the celebrated and unfortunate James Sharp, created Primate of Scotland on the revival of the prelacy after the Restoration. The prelates of the old Scottish Church and a Presbyterian of the original leaven would give very different interpretations of the emblems which can be traced upon his chimney grate. The motto is 'FIDES DONA SUPERAT,' illustrated by the figure of a muffled man; that is, a ruffian having his cloak so closely wrapped about him as to disguise his features, who is offering to bribe with meat a mastiff dog, which sturdily rejects the temptation." The headings represent respectively: (1) design from the back of an antique chair at Abbotsford; (2) the carvings on the two presses in the front hall made from Erskine's pulpit; (3) designs from the wood carvings in the small turret off the study, familiarly called "Speak a bit"; and (4) the delicate stone carvings which ornament the garden screen. Of these, two only perhaps are deserving of special remark. The carving from the little turret claims to be part of Queen Mary's bed, used by her during her visits to Jedburgh, where the house occupied by her may still be visited, and was no doubt the scene of the Queen's dangerous illness thus described by Mr. Hosack: "While the court was still at Jedburgh (October 1566) the Queen was seized with a dangerous fever, the result, according to the opinion of Maitland, of the continual vexation and anxiety which she suffered through the perverse conduct of her husband. For more than a week her life was in imminent peril, and she awaited the result with characteristic fortitude and resignation. She earnestly recommended her son to the Earl of Moray, and exhorted him and his brother nobles to live in peace. She declared her intention of dying in the religion in which she had been brought up; and she besought her brother not to deal harshly with her Catholic subjects after she was gone." [1]

The stone foliage from the garden screen is copied from similar carvings at Melrose Abbey, and brings to our minds the exquisite descriptions in the *Lay of the Last Minstrel.*

" By foliaged tracery combined ;
Thou would'st have thought some fairy's hand
'Twixt poplars straight the ozier wand
In many a freakish knot had twined ;
Then framed a spell, when the work was done,
And changed the willow wreath to stone."

In conclusion, I would wish to express my warm thanks for the kind and courteous assistance I have received from Mr. William Gibb and other friends, in my endeavour to describe "Abbotsford and its Treasures."

M. M. MAXWELL SCOTT.

Note.—The references to Mr. Lockhart's *Life of Scott* are applicable to the last (and present) edition in ten volumes, which also corresponds with the Royal 8vo edition in one volume.

---

[1] *Mary Queen of Scots and her Accusers*, by John Hosack, vol. i. p. 161, 2nd ed. (William Blackwood and Sons). See also *Memorials of Mary Stuart*, by Claude Nau.

PLATE I

SIR WALTER SCOTT'S DESK AND CHAIR

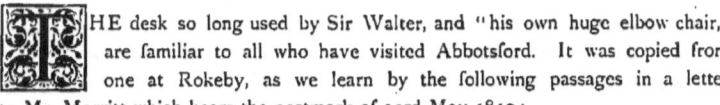HE desk so long used by Sir Walter, and "his own huge elbow chair," are familiar to all who have visited Abbotsford. It was copied from one at Rokeby, as we learn by the following passages in a letter to Mr. Morritt which bears the postmark of 23rd May 1810 :—

"I have a little commission for you if you will be kind enough to accept of it. You know I fell in love with your library table, and now that the 'Lady' has put crowns into my purse I would willingly treat myself to the like. Only I think I have not much occasion for the space which holds accompt-books ; in other respects it is quite a model, and in that respect I don't quarrel with it, for why should I not be a rich man some day and have accompt-books? And therefore I intrude so far on your time as to request you when you are taking a walk to order me such a table as yours."

The desk cannot be better described than in Mr. Lockhart's words. They relate to it as he first saw it in the "Den" in Castle Street in 1818.

"The only table was a massive piece of furniture which he had had constructed on the model of one at Rokeby ; with a desk and all its appurtenances on either side, that an amanuensis might work opposite to him when he chose ; and with small tiers of drawers, reaching all round to the floor. The top displayed a goodly array of session papers, and on the desk below were, besides the MS. at which he was

I

working, sundry parcels of letters, proof-sheets, and so forth, all neatly done up with red tape. His own writing apparatus was a very handsome old box, richly carved, lined with crimson velvet, and containing ink-bottles, taper-stand, etc., in silver, the whole in such order that it might have come from the silversmith's window half an hour before."

And again what can be more pathetic than Mr. Lockhart's description of the opening of the desk on that sad day fourteen years later ?

"But perhaps the most touching evidence of the lasting tenderness of Sir Walter's early domestic feelings was exhibited to his executors when they opened his repositories in search of his testament, the evening after his burial. On lifting up his desk, we found arranged in careful order a series of little objects which had obviously been so placed there that his eye might rest on them every morning before he began his tasks. These were the old-fashioned boxes that had garnished his mother's toilette, when he, a sickly child, slept in her dressing-room—the silver taper-stand which the young advocate had bought for her with his first five guinea fee—a row of small packets inscribed with her hand, and containing the hair of those of her offspring that had died before her—his father's snuff-box and étui case, and more things of the like sort, recalling

'The old familiar faces.'"

PANELS FROM ERSKINE'S PULPIT

PLATE II

HALL DOOR LOOKING TOWARDS STUDY AND
SHOWING CORNER OF DESK

N the *Reliquiæ* Sir Walter thus describes this end of the hall :—" The eastern end of this room is fashioned into two niches, modelled in Paris plaster from those splendid sculptured niches which formerly held the Saints and Apostles of the Abbey of Melrose. These niches are each of them occupied by what is very rarely seen in Scotland, namely a complete suit of feudal steel armour." [1] In the hands of the figure to the left is placed "a sword nearly six feet in length, and wielded with both hands. This we must consider as the *gladius militis levis armaturæ*, or the sword of the light-armed soldier. It was with such weapons that men in old times fought at barriers or passes, in the natural straits of a mountainous country, or upon the breach of a defended castle. They are found mentioned in the wars of Switzerland, and in the feuds of the Scottish clans. The Scottish poet Barbour gives a most interesting account of the successful defence made by his hero (Bruce) against the vassals of John of Lorn, three of whom, armed with these dreadful weapons, attacked the monarch at once after the rout of Dalry, and were all slain by him. [2]

[1] The suit of armour is 6 ft. in height, the sword 6 ft. 7 in. in length, the blade 3 in. broad, the grip 20 in. The helmet measures 31 in. round at widest part.

[2] " Thai saw on syd thre men cummand,
  Lik to lycht men and wanerand ;
  Swerdis thai had, and axys als."
        (Barbour, *The Bruce*, Book v. verse 410.)

"There are several swords of the kind in my small collection . . . but none of them are like that placed in the grasp of the warrior of Bosworth, which, to speak the truth, may match even with the tremendous blade of the Castle of Otranto."

It was through these doors that Mr. Lockhart wheeled Sir Walter for his last visit to the study, so touchingly described in the *Life*.

These doorways are also connected with the story of Lord Byron's supposed apparition to Sir Walter, soon after his death. (August 1827.)

Those who have seen Abbotsford will remember that there is at the end of the hall, opposite to the entrance of the library, an arched doorway leading to other rooms. One night some of the party observed that, by an arrangement of light, easily to be imagined, a luminous space was formed upon the library door, in which the shadow of a person standing in the opposite archway made a very imposing appearance, the body of the hall remaining quite dark. Sir Walter had some time before told his friends of the deception of sight (mentioned in his *Demonology*) which made him for a moment imagine a figure of Lord Byron standing in the same hall. We quote Sir Walter's words—"Not long after the death of a late illustrious poet who had filled, while living, a great station in the eye of the public, a literary friend, to whom the deceased had been well known, was engaged during the darkening twilight of an autumn evening in perusing one of the publications which professed to detail the habits and opinions of the distinguished individual who was now no more. As the reader had enjoyed the intimacy of the deceased to a considerable degree, he was deeply interested in the publication, which contained some particulars relating to himself and other friends. A visitor was sitting in the apartment who was also engaged in reading. Their sitting-room opened into an entrance-hall, rather fantastically fitted up with articles of armour, skins of wild animals, and the like. It was when laying down his book, and passing into this hall, through which the moon was beginning to shine, that the individual of whom I speak saw, right before him, and in a standing posture, the exact representation of his departed friend, whose recollection had been so strongly brought to his imagination. He stopped for a single moment, so as to notice the wonderful accuracy with which fancy had impressed upon the bodily eye the peculiarities of dress and posture of the illustrious poet. Sensible, however, of the delusion, he felt no sentiment save that of wonder at the extraordinary accuracy of the resemblance, and stepped onwards towards the figure, which resolved itself, as he approached, into the various materials of which it was composed. These were merely a screen, occupied by great-coats, shawls, plaids, and such other articles as usually are found in a country entrance-hall. The spectator returned to the spot from which he had seen the illusion, and endeavoured with all his power to recall the image which had been so singularly vivid. But this was beyond his capacity ; and the person who had witnessed the apparition, or, more properly, whose excited state had been the means of raising it, had only to return into the apartment, and tell his young friend under what a striking hallucination he had for a moment laboured." [1]

[1] Scott's Prose Works, *Letters on Demonology and Witchcraft.*

PLATE III

STAIRCASE IN THE STUDY

IN the *Reliquiæ Trottcosianæ* Sir Walter describes the study and its stair-case as follows:—

"The study is a private apartment 16 feet high, like the others, 20 feet long by about 14 broad, with a space of about 7 feet in height to the ceiling of the apartment, which affords room for a small gallery filled up with oaken shelves running round three sides of the study, and resting upon small projecting beams of oak. The gallery and its contents are accessible by a small stair, about 3 feet in breadth, which gains room to ascend in the southward angle of the chamber and runs in front of the books, leaving such a narrow passage as is sometimes found in front of the balustrades of old convents, and was certainly designed for the use of the lay brethren alone. In the south-east angle of the room a small door encloses a stair-case which leads about seven paces higher, and by another private entrance reaches the bedroom story of the house, and lands in the proprietor's dressing-room. The inhabitant of the study, therefore, if unwilling to be surprised by visitors, may make his retreat unobserved by means of this gallery to the private staircase which unites his study with his bedroom,—a facility which he has sometimes found extremely convenient."

In the bookcase under the stair may be observed some of the volumes of the *Moniteur*, used for consultation by Sir Walter when he was engaged on the *Life of Napoleon*. The chair called "The Wallace Chair," presented by Joseph Train to Sir Walter in 1822, is made from the only remaining wood of the house of

Robroyston, the traditionary scene of betrayal of Sir William Wallace. "It is generally said that he was made prisoner at Robroyston, near Glasgow, and the tradition of the country bears that the signal for rushing upon him and taking him unawares was when one of his pretended friends who betrayed him should turn a loaf, which was placed upon the table, with its bottom or flat side uppermost."[1]

[1] *Tales of a Grandfather*, vol. i. p. 55, Edin. 1836.

PLATE IV

THE DINING-ROOM

HIS room, his "own great parlour," is thus described by Sir Walter :—
"The eating room is a quiet apartment; not very large indeed, yet ample
enough for all the common wants and purposes. The ceiling is not above
12 feet in height, and is apparently supported by ribs of carved oak, which neverthe-
less are only stucco, but so ingeniously moulded and painted and hid with escutcheons
at the places where they cross each other, that they can hardly be distinguished from
the more permanent material." [1]

This apartment has for us now a special and solemn interest, as it was here that
Sir Walter died. When he returned from his last sad journey, on 9th July 1832, the
dining-room was arranged as his bedroom, and although at first he was able to be
wheeled about the house, and also out of doors, after the 17th he appears never to
have left this room.

"As I was dressing on the morning of the 17th of September," writes Mr.
Lockhart, "Nicolson came into my room and told me that his master had awoke in
a state of composure and consciousness, and wished to see me immediately. I found
him entirely himself, though in the last extreme of feebleness. His eye was clear
and calm—every trace of the wild fire of delirium extinguished. 'Lockhart,' he
said, 'I may have but a minute to speak to you. My dear, be a good man—be
virtuous, be religious, be a good man. Nothing else will give you any comfort when
you come to lie here.' He paused, and I said, 'Shall I send for Sophia and

[1] *Reliquiæ.*

2

Anne?' 'No,' said he, 'don't disturb them. Poor souls! I know they were up all night. God bless you all.' With this he sank into a very tranquil sleep, and indeed, he scarcely afterwards gave any sign of consciousness, except for an instant on the arrival of his sons. They, on learning that the scene was about to close, obtained a new leave of absence from their posts, and both reached Abbotsford on the 19th. About half-past 1 P.M. on the 21st September Sir Walter breathed 'his last, in the presence of all his children. It was a beautiful day,—so warm that every window was wide open—and so perfectly still that the sound of all others most delicious to his ear, the gentle ripple of the Tweed over its pebbles, was distinctly audible as we knelt around the bed, and his eldest son kissed and closed his eyes."

Among the flags placed in the corner of the room may be observed one of dark blue silk, having in gold letters "L'Empereur Napoleon au 105me Regiment d'Infanterie de Ligne," which Sir Walter probably acquired at the same time as the other Waterloo treasures. There is an interesting reference to its possible history in a letter of Colonel A. K. Clark Kennedy, relating to the Battle of Waterloo, lately published,[1] in which he describes capturing a French Eagle belonging to the 105th French Regiment. "I did not," says the letter, "see the Eagle and the colours (for there were two colours, but only one with an Eagle) until we had been probably five or six minutes engaged." The Eagle and its colours were taken, and the letter proceeds: "What became of the other colours without the Eagle I know not, but it is rather singular that I last autumn saw a dark blue silk flag, with the words 105me Regiment d'Infanterie de Ligne in gold letters upon it, in the hall at Abbotsford along with other military curiosities. How it got there I could not learn, the present Sir Walter Scott telling me he had no knowledge of how it got into his late father's possession, or where it came from. Could this have been the very flag that was along with the Eagle, or was it only a camp colour ? The flag of the Eagle was red, white, and blue, this is all blue."

[1] Waterloo Letters, edited by Major-General H. T. Siborne, London 1891, pp. 75, 76.

STONE CARVINGS FROM GARDEN SCREEN

PLATE V

SIR WALTER SCOTT'S BODY CLOTHES
COAT, WAISTCOAT, HAT, AND WALKING-STICK

HE coat is of dark green broad-cloth, with white metal buttons. It has a deep, straight, turned-down collar, and is a "cut away coat." The cuffs are made tight to button.

The waistcoat is of narrow cream and black stripe in silk, with yellow metal buttons.

The tall hat is a beaver, with flat brim, and of a pale fawn colour.

Walking-stick, with brown leather sheath on the point, evidently to prevent slipping on the smooth floor.

These clothes may very probably be the same as those worn by Sir Walter when he sat for his last portrait, a few months before his death. This little sketch (for the young artist, Mr. Edmonstone, did not live to paint the projected picture) represents Sir Walter seated in an arm-chair. He holds his stick in his left hand; his daughter Anne, and a young friend, Miss M'Kenzie, are also included in the drawing. The date "Rome, April 23rd, 1832," is written above, and the artist has also jotted down the colour of the clothes worn by Sir Walter thus: "Bottle-green coat, light waistcoat, etc."

PLATE VI

SIR WALTER SCOTT'S PIPES, SPECTACLES
AND CASE, AND PAPER-CUTTER

SIR WALTER'S pipes are finely coloured meerschaums, mounted in silver and with silver covers. The larger one has a perforated ornament round the cover with stem of cherry wood and cord and tassels of black and gold. The smaller pipe has a silver cleaner attached by a chain, and the initials W. S. and Abbotsford engraved on the cover.

The paper-knife is of ivory with a scroll and foliage design on one panel of the handle. A woodland scene with stag is carved on the other.

The spectacles are of tortoise-shell with red leather case. These gabions are drawn nearly full size.

PLATE VII

PRUNING-KNIFE, MALLET, CHISEL, WHITE TAIL
MOUNTED IN ANTIQUE SILVER HANDLE

I

HIS knife is a strong double-bladed knife, with deer-horn handle, in length 6 inches. It has the following interesting story connected with it.

In the autumn of 1815, on his return from France, Sir Walter and Mr. Scott of Gala travelled together to Scotland.

"They spent a night at Sheffield, and early next morning Sir Walter sallied forth to provide himself with a planter's knife of the most complex contrivance and finished workmanship. Having secured one to his mind, and which for many years after was his constant pocket companion, he wrote his name on a card: 'Walter Scott, Abbotsford,' and directed it to be engraved on the handle. On his mentioning this acquisition at breakfast, young Gala expressed his desire to equip himself in like fashion, and was directed to the shop accordingly. When he had purchased a similar knife, and produced his name in turn for the engraver, the master-cutter eyed the signature for a moment and exclaimed, 'John Scott of Gala. Well! I hope your ticket may serve me in as good stead as another Mr. Scott's has just done. Upon my word, one of my best men, an honest fellow from the north, went out of his senses when he saw it. He offered me a week's work if I would let him keep it to

himself—and I took Saunders at his word!' Scott used to talk of this as one of
the most gratifying compliments he ever received in his literary capacity." [1]

II

The chisel is $14\frac{1}{4}$ inches over all, the blade being 9 in. long and 2 in. at its
broadest part.   The mallet and chisel are hung in strong leather cases to a broad
strap and buckle.

III

The white tail mounted in silver was used by Sir Walter for dusting his books.
The handle is 14 inches in length.

[1] *Life* (in 10 vols.), vol. v, pp. 88, 89.

PANELS FROM ERSKINE'S PULPIT

PLATE VIII

A PURSE WORN BY SIR WALTER SCOTT

HIS purse, which is much worn, is made of mole-skin of a dark grey colour. The clasp is silver with ornament in strong relief. The outline of the clasp is varied by curves, and there is a double curve at the corners. The skin is fastened to the clasp by silver pins, and the purse shuts with a spring lever and catch, and is opened by pressing two silver pins close to the hinges.

The purse has two pockets, and is lined with pale yellow kid; the central division has been renewed and bound with pale red ribbon.

The plate shows the purse both open and shut—both views being drawn full size.

It contains a piece of paper on which is written : " An old purse worn by Sir Walter Scott for many years, made of mole-skin."

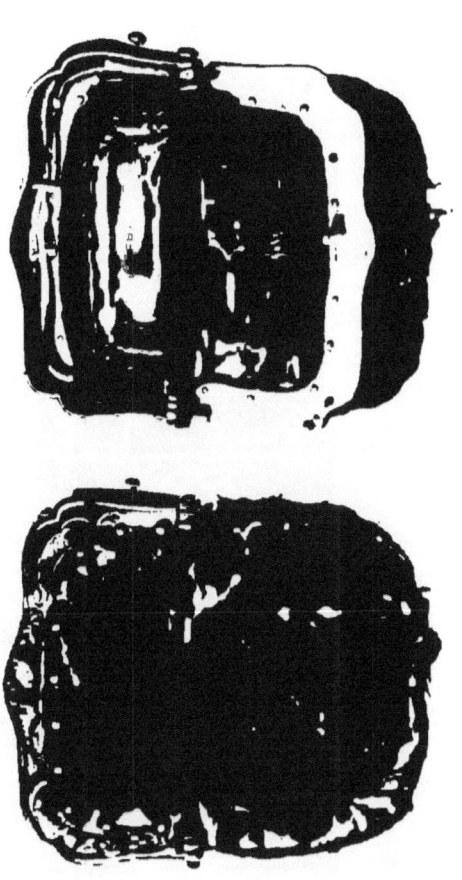

PLATE IX

MONTROSE'S SWORD

"I'll make thee glorious by my pen
And famous by my sword."—MONTROSE.

THIS gabion, which we venture to consider as perhaps the most precious in Sir Walter's collection, was given by Charles I. to his faithful follower. Unfortunately no record of the gift, or of the occasion of it, can be found in the history of Montrose. Sir Walter himself tells us how the sword came into his possession. " I have moreover," he writes, "a relic of a more heroic character ; it is a sword which was given to the great Marquis of Montrose by Charles I., and appears to have belonged to his father, our gentle King Jamie. It has been preserved for a long time at Gartmore, but the present proprietor was selling his library, or great part of it, and John Ballantyne the purchaser, wishing to oblige me, would not conclude a bargain which the gentleman's necessity made him anxious about till he flung the sword into the scale. It is, independent of its other merits, a most beautiful blade. I think a Dialogue between the same sword and Rob Roy's gun might be composed with good effect." ·

This sword, fit emblem of the task undertaken by the "great Marquis" for his royal master, suggests to us many memories of the owner, that "mirror of chivalry" of whom a foreign contemporary[1] says that he was "the only man in the world who has ever realised to me the ideas of certain heroes whom we now discover nowhere

[1] Cardinal de Retz.

but in the *Lives* of Plutarch," and whom another contemporary—a countryman of his own—has thus affectionately described : "And it cannot be denyed but he was ane accomplished gentleman of many excellent partes, a bodie not tall, but comely, and well compossed in all his liniamentes ; his complexion meerly white, with flaxin haire ; of a stayed, graue, and solide looke, and yet eyes sparkling and full of lyfe ; of speach slow, but wittie and full of sence ; a presence graitfull, courtly, and so winneing upon the beholder, as it seemed to claim reuerence without seweing for it ; for he was so affable, so courteous, so bening as seemed verely to scorn ostentation and the keeping of state, and therfor he quicklie made a conquesse of the heartes of all his followers, so as whan he list he could haue lead them in a chaine to haue followed him with chearefullnes in all his interpryses ; and I am certainely perswaded that this his gratious, humane, and courteous fredome of behaviour being certanely acceptable befor God as well as men, was it that wanne him so much renovne, and inabled him chiefly, in the loue of his followers, to goe through so great interprysses wheirin his equall had failled, although they exceeded him farre in power, nor can any other reason be given for it but only this. . . .

"I thinke veralie he was naturally inclyned to humilitie, courtesie, gentlenes, and freedome of cariage. He did not seeme to affect state nor to claim reuerence, nor to keep a distance with gentlemen that ware not his domestickes ; but rather in a noble yet courteouse way he seemed to slight those vanisheing smockes of greatnes, affecting rather the reall possession of men's heartes than the frothie and outward showe of reuerence ; and therefor was all reuerence thrust upon him, because all did loue him, therfor all did honour him and reuerence him, yea, haueing once acquired there heartes, they were readie not only to honour him, but to quarrell with any that would not honour him ; and would not spare their fortounes, nor derest blood about there heartes ; to the end he might be honoured because they saue that he tooke the right course to obtaine honour. He had fund furth the right way to be reuerenced, and thereby was approued that propheticke maxime which hath neuer failed, nor neuer shall faille, being pronounced by the Fountaine of truth." ("He that humbleth himself shall be exalted.") [1]

The sword bears on both sides the Royal Arms of Great Britain. The following inscription is also engraved on the blade—

[1] *A short abridgement of Britane's Distemper*, etc., by Patrick Gordon of Ruthven, 1639-49, pp. 76-78. (Printed for the Spalding Club.)

JACOBE ALUMNE PACIS ATK PALLAE
SERENE CULTOR ET DECUS BRITANNICI
CLARISSIMUM REGNI TUIS REGALID
SCEPTRIS SUDEST DE STIRPE QUOND MARTIA.

The sword measures about 34 inches in length, the blade being 27 and the hilt 7 inches. The blade is straight and two-edged, beautifully ornamented ; the hilt, open scroll work and silver gilt ; the grip, bound with alternate chains of silver and flat bands of gold. The sheath was remounted by Sir Walter's order in 1822.

In the drawing the sword is represented half real size, with inscription and arms full size.

PLATE X

PAIR OF PISTOLS WHICH BELONGED TO NAPOLEON I.[1]

THESE pistols were taken from the Emperor's carriage after the Battle of Waterloo. The barrels are octagonal and rifled, and enlarge slightly towards the muzzle. They bear the inscription : " Boutel Directeur Artiste, No. 97. Manufacture à Versailles," and the letters " B.C. N.B." The barrels have five bands of small gold dots. The stocks are cross hatched in panels with fine lines, and all the mountings are beautifully engraved and enriched with filigree ornament.

SIR WALTER SCOTT'S VOLUNTEER PISTOLS

The pair of pistols used by Sir Walter as yeoman in the Edinburgh Volunteer Cavalry are unrifled and bear the name " D. Egg, London." Also the letters " G. R." and a royal crown. Butts obtusely rounded. Barrel 9 in. Stock 8 in. Mounted with brass.

PISTOL WHICH BELONGED TO CLAVERHOUSE

Claverhouse's pistol is a fine old Highland pistol, with barrel partly rounded and partly octagonal. It is ornamented with inlaid lines of gold, and bands and

[1] Mr. Lockhart believed that these pistols were presented to Sir Walter by Col. the Hon. James Stanhope.

plates of silver, finely chased. The butt of the pistol is lobated, and the trigger ends in a rounded knob.

It is unfortunately not known how Claverhouse's pistol came into Sir Walter's possession, nor are we aware of any story connected with the hero and this weapon.

OLD PISTOL BY CAMPBELL OF DOUNE

This is a fine old Highland pistol bearing the maker's name, "John Campbell, Doune." It is of steel beautifully inlaid with silver, and both metals are elaborately engraved. The barrel is partly round and partly octagonal, and widens slightly towards the muzzle. The whole pistol is beautifully chased with foliage and scroll ornament.

PISTOL WHICH BELONGED TO SIR WALTER SCOTT

This pistol is one of a pair which belonged to Sir Walter. It has an oval plate inlaid in the stock, and bears his arms. The maker's name, "Macleod," is engraved on the lock. The lower and upper parts of the stock are crossed by narrow bands of silver, separating panels beautifully engraved with foliage in low relief. The barrel is round at the breech, but polygonal, and enlarging slightly towards the muzzle. The stock has panels with diaper pattern, and the end of trigger and head of picker bear each a cross in narrow bands of silver.

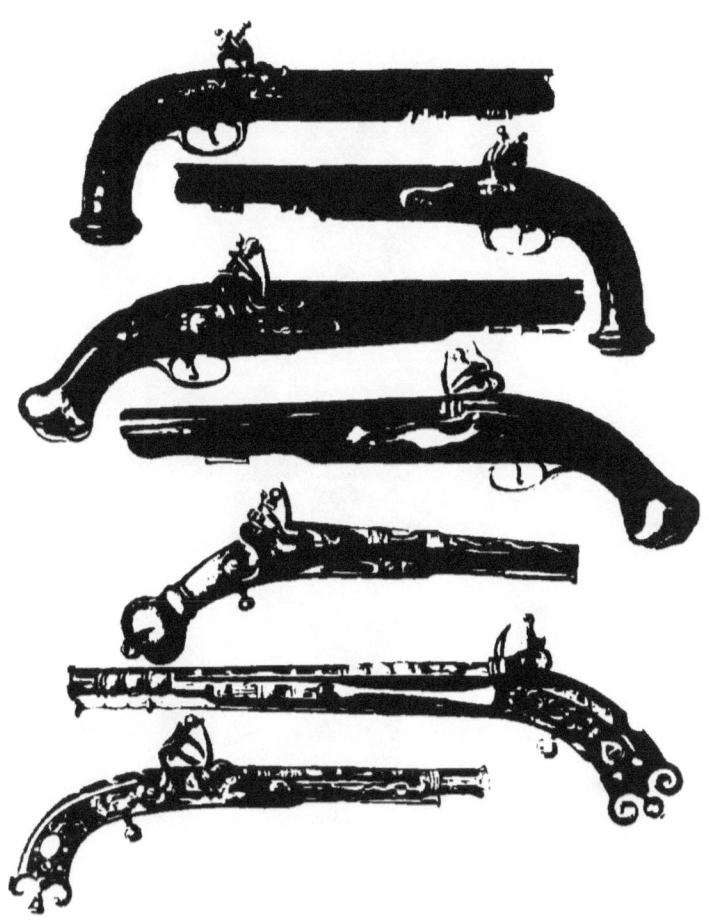

PLATE XI

ENLARGED DRAWING OF ARMOUR FROM HALL DOOR

HE description of this gabion given by Sir Walter is so connected with the story of a companion suit of armour that we venture to give the passage referring to both. The cuirass represented in this drawing belongs to the second in order of description.

"The one was designed for a French knight, one of the gendarmes of the Middle Ages. He must have been a man considerably under the middle size, and the suit of armour exhibits one peculiarity which will be interesting to students of the learned Dr. Meyrick. The shield, which is very rarely the companion of the suit of armour, is not only present in this case, but secured in an unusual manner by nails, with large screw heads, instead of being hung round the neck, as was common during 'a career,' the hands being thus left free, the right to manage the lance, the left to hold the horse's bridle. To complete this suit of armour a lance is placed in one hand exactly after the measure of one in Dr. Meyrick's collection. In the other hand is a drawn sword, which is carved over with writing, and contrived so as to keep a record of the days of the Catholic saints. In a word, it is a calendar to direct the good knight's devotions. *The other suit of armour*, which is also complete in all its parts, was said when it came into my possession to have belonged to a knight who took arms upon Richmond's side at the field of Bosworth, and died, I think, of his wounds there. If one were disposed to give him a name, the size of his armour might suggest that he was Sir John Cheney, the biggest man of both armies on that memorable day. I venture to think—for I feel myself gliding into the prosy style of an antiquarian, disposed in sailor phrase to spin a tough yarn—I venture to think that the calendar placed in the hand of the little French knight originally belonged to the gigantic warrior of Bosworth Field. I imagine it was withdrawn for the purpose of supplying its place with a noble specimen of the sword of the Swiss mountaineers." [1]

The cuirass measures 47 in. round the chest and 37 in. round the waist.

[1] In the drawing the calendar sword is placed in the warrior's hand according to Sir Walter's suggestion.

PLATE XII

NAPOLEON'S PEN-CASE AND BLOTTING-BOOK

APOLEON'S pen-case is a small box, oblong in shape, $1\frac{1}{8}$ inch in width by 8 inches in length, and 1 inch in depth. It is covered with green silk velvet, lined with green satin. On the top is the initial N in gold wire surrounded by a laurel wreath. The sides of the box are ornamented with a double line of flat gold ribbon (or lace) crossed by the gold wire. It contains a stick of red sealing-wax partly used, and a paper with the following lines:—"This sealing-wax was left by Napoleon on his writing-table in the Palace of the Elysée Bourbon the morning he fled from Paris, after the Cent Jours, in 1815, probably the last he used as Emperor. Given to *Vis⁴⁵ Hampden* by *Mme La Duchesse de Goutaut.* With Lady Hampden's compts. to Sir Walter Scott, July 1829."

The little paper in the pen-box tells the story of the sealing-wax, but whether the case itself was found at the Elysée Bourbon is uncertain. It would appear to belong to the same writing-set as the blotting-book described below. In connection with Napoleon's melancholy residence at the Elysée Bourbon after his great defeat, and during the last days of his liberty, Lt.-Colonel Charras, in his *Histoire de la Campagne de* 1815, makes the following interesting remarks:—

"At four o'clock in the morning Napoleon had arrived . . . not at the Tuileries, but at the Elysée Bourbon, as if he had realised that defeat closed for him the brilliant palace where his vanity had so delighted in exhibiting all the pomp of the monarchy of Louis XIV.," and again: "After having allowed an unwilling abdication to be extorted from him, he had remained in close retirement in the Palace of the Elysée Bourbon. . . ." After waiting for three days in the vain hope that his crown might be again offered him, "he was obliged to cede to the injunctions, little softened in form, which Fouché sent him, expressing the will of the Chambers; and he established himself at Malmaison, his former residence, the residence of the First Consul, and of the victor of Marengo!!"

Napoleon's blotting-book—10½ inches long by 8½ and 1 inch thick—is covered with the same coloured green silk velvet as the pen-case, and lined with the same satin. It is tied with three pairs of greenish-blue ribbons, fringed with gold beads, and passing through a hollow ball of gold filigree so as to form a sort of tassel. The same ribbon passes down the back to form a holder for the blotting-paper, but is now torn.

Both sides are alike ornamented with the initial N in the centre, surmounted by an imperial crown, and having beneath it a semicircular wreath of laurel. There are bees in each corner, and scrolls of carved foliage are joined in pairs by rosette or sunflower ornaments in the centre of each side. The extreme corners have four of the same ornaments slightly modified in form, and the whole is surrounded by a border of the flat lace bound down at intervals by triple lines, and having the corners ornamented by a trefoil. The whole elaborate embroidery is in different forms of gold wire.

The tradition regarding this gabion is that it was found in Napoleon's carriage after the battle of Waterloo. There are various interesting references to the Emperor's carriage and its contents in the annals of Waterloo; and, although the portfolio is not mentioned, we venture to quote from them. Colonel Charras and Blücher himself both allude to the subject. The former says that "a considerable number of artillery carriages and others were taken by the Prussians at and near Genappe, and the greater part of the equipages belonging to the generals of Napoleon and his suite, and the carriage itself in which he had come from Paris, which had escaped in the disasters of Russia, and contained clothes and a sword belonging to the vanquished." [1]

Blücher, writing to his wife, uses words to this effect :—

"GOSSLIER, *June 25th*, 1815.

"Napoleon got off in the night without hat or sword. His hat and sword I

---

[1] Fleury de Chaboulon says that there was also in the carriage "the superb diamond necklace that the Princess Borghese (Pauline Bonaparte) had given to Napoleon." What became of it we know not.

send to-day to the king. His extremely rich mantle of state and *his carriage* are in my hands, and I also possess his field-glass, through which he looked at us on the day of the battle ;[1] the carriage I will send you, only it is a pity that it is injured . . . . he was about to retreat in his carriage, and when he was surprised by my troops, he jumped out, threw himself on horseback without his sword, when his hat tumbled off. . . .[2]

The portfolio contains a small packet of Napoleon's hair accompanied by the following letter addressed to Mrs. Hughes,[3] Rev. Dr. Hughes, Amen Corner, St. Paul's :--

NETHER HALL,
Nov. 8th, 1827.

MY DEAR MADAM,

I avail myself of the opportunity afforded me by Miss Hyde's going to town to send an article of some curiosity which I wish to present, through you, to Sir Walter Scott. It is a small piece of Buonaparte's hair. I came by it in the following manner. My friend Captain Haviside was the bearer of certain presents from Mr. Elphinstone, a gentleman filling a high official situation in China, to the exiled Emperor, who had on some occasion shown either polite or humane attentions —I believe the latter—to Mr. Elphinstone's brother, an officer in the British army. On leaving these presents at St. Helena, Captain Haviside obtained a pass for Longwood, and went there for the express purpose of having an audience of the Emperor. He, the Emperor, was ill and could not receive him, but he was entertained by his suite, and Mme. Bertrand gave him a small quantity of the Emperor's hair, which she had obtained from his valet a few days before. This quantity, small originally, has diminished hair by hair, to gratify the curiosity of the officers of the ship, until the portion I now send you was all that remained. I am sorry it is so small, but it is all I have ; and if you do not think Sir Walter will be offended by the liberty I take in offering it to him, I shall be much obliged if you will present

---

[1] "Napoleon had hitherto maintained his usual serenity of aspect, on the heights of La Belle Alliance. He watched the English onset with his *spy-glass*—became suddenly pale as death—exclaimed, 'They are mingled together—all is lost for the present,' and rode off the field." *History of Napoleon Buonaparte*, by J. G. Lockhart, p. 320. London, John Murray, 1835.

[2] Blücher, *Briefe aus den Feldzügen* 1813-1815. Herausgegeben von E. von Colomb, Stuttgart, 1876.

[3] Mrs. Hughes was a friend of Sir Walter's. She was introduced to him in 1807 by Mrs. Hayman, Privy-Purse to Queen Caroline.

it to him in my name. I would that I had some more valuable offering by which I could testify my gratitude for the many hours of delight he has afforded me ; and yet, feeling as I do that I am already more than repaid for this or anything I could give him, I still crave something in return, and that something is an acknowledgment of the receipt of my trifle in his own handwriting. I shall value it more than the hair, or even than the head of any emperor that ever existed. With my best regards to. Dr. Hughes, believe me to remain, dear Madam, very sincerely yours,

R. DALTON.

P.S.—O'Meara's book contains an account of Captain Haviside's visit, but it is false throughout. A pass to Longwood was given to Captain Haviside by Sir H. Lowe without hesitation, and without any caution or condition whatever. being annexed.

FROM BACK OF A CHAIR AT ABBOTSFORD

PLATE XIII

WATERLOO CUIRASSES AND SWORD

" My steel-clad cuirasseers advance,
Each Hulan forward with his lance,
My guard—my chosen,—charge for France,
France and Napoleon.

Rushed on the ponderous cuirasseer,
The lancer couched his ruthless spear,
And hurrying as to havoc near
The cohorts' eagles flew."

(*The Field of Waterloo.*—SIR W. SCOTT.)

HESE spoils from Napoleon's army were secured by Sir Walter on the occasion of his visit to the field of Waterloo. In Major Pryse Gordon's account of this visit he tells us that "when Sir Walter had examined every point of defence and attack, we adjourned to the 'Original Duke of Wellington' at Waterloo, to lunch after the fatigues of the ride. Here we had a crowded levee of peasants, and collected a great many trophies, from *cuirasses* down to buttons and bullets."

We also find references to the cuirasses both in the *Reliquiæ* and in *Paul's Letters*. In the former, Sir Walter, in describing the hall, says : " Before I quit the hall, I ought to say that the end on the west, or left side of the entrance, is garnished with spoils from the field of Waterloo, where I collected them in person, very

shortly after that memorable action. There are two or three cuirasses both of brass
and steel. The cuirasses of the former metal are become very rare because they
were at once knocked to pieces by the peasantry, who could sell the copper of which
they were made at so much a pound. The belts, swords, and axes of the train are
also come to anchor in this whimsical place."

In *Paul's Letters* Sir Walter enters into further details as follows : " The great
object of ambition was to possess the armour of a cuirasseer, which at first might
have been bought in great quantity, almost all the *wearers* having fallen in that
bloody battle—the victors have indeed carried off some of these cuirasses, to serve
as culinary vessels, and I myself have seen the Highlanders frying their rations of
beef or mutton upon the breast-plates and back-pieces of their discomfited adversaries.
But enough remained to make the fortunes of the people of St. John, Waterloo,
Planchenoit, etc. When I was at La Belle Alliance I bought the cuirass of a common
soldier for about 6 francs, but a very handsome inlaid one, once the property of a
French officer of distinction, which was for sale in Brussels, cost me four times that
sum. As for the casques, or head-pieces, which by the way are remarkably handsome,
they are almost *introuvable*. For the peasants almost immediately sold them to be
beat out for old copper ; and the purchaser, needlessly afraid of their being reclaimed,
destroyed them as fast as possible."

The steel cuirass measures 3 feet 2 inches round the waist, and 3 feet
6½ inches round the chest.

The brass cuirass is 3 feet 3½ inches round waist, 3 feet 6½ inches round chest.

The sword-blade measures 38 inches in length, the breadth at hilt 1½ inch,
and the hilt itself 6¾ inches. The grip is covered with black leather bound with
brass wire. The guard is formed of flat brass bands.

The helmet measures 16 inches in height, and 8 inches from back to front. The
upper half of the helmet is of bright steel, with the crest in brass, and is highly
ornamented at the side with foliage and fluting. The horse-hair plume is about
2 feet in length.

PANELS FROM ERSKINE'S PULPIT

PLATE XIV

QUEEN MARY'S SEAL

THIS ornament, commonly called Queen Mary's Seal, is in silver-gilt, decorated with foliage and shell work in high relief. It is 3 inches high by 1½ inch broad, and forms a double box, of which the upper half was possibly used as a vinaigrette. The base is engraved with a crowned shield bearing the ruddy lion of Scotland and the initials M. R.

TRICOLOURED COCKADE

The cockade, which is drawn full size, is made of a straight piece of broad ribbon striped in red, white, and blue, drawn together in the centre so as to form a rosette. The tricolour, emblematic of the great Revolution, was designed by General Lafayette, and was at first the badge of the National Guard. These colours were adopted by France as the national colours in 1789. Red and blue were selected as the arms of Paris, and the white was added as the colour of the monarchy and the army, and to show the intimate union which should exist between the people and the armed force.

It is probable that Sir Walter brought this gabion back from France in 1815. As illustrating the use of the tricolour by one of Napoleon's old soldiers we quote the following amusing paragraph from Sir Walter's account of his visit to Valenciennes in the same year.

"There was, however, in the air and eye of the soldiers of Buonaparte (for such these military men still call themselves) something of pride and self-elation, that

5

indicated undaunted confidence in their own skill and valour. They appeared, however, disunited and disorganised. Some wore the white cockade, others still displayed the tricolour, and one prudent fellow had, for his own amusement and that of his comrades, stuck both in his hat at once, so as to make a *cocarde de convenance*, which might suit either party that should get uppermost."

PURSE GIVEN TO SIR WALTER SCOTT BY JOANNA BAILLIE

This purse, made by the poetess for Sir Walter, is netted in thick red silk. It has a silver clasp with grotesque figures in high relief. A thistle projects from the top of the clasp and forms part of the spring catch. The purse is finished by a tassel of silver chains, ending with small flat plates which are fastened into a silver cup-shaped end.

As is well known, a long and intimate friendship subsisted between Sir Walter and the amiable and gifted Joanna Baillie, whose dramatic poems he greatly admired. Miss Baillie was born at the Manse of Bothwell in 1762, and lived to a great age, dying in 1851. She was sister of the well-known Dr. Matthew Baillie. In order to be near him Miss Baillie and her sister Agnes settled in London, where their cottage at Hampstead became the centre of a brilliant literary society. In 1798 Joanna published her first volume of the *Plays on the Passions*. These Plays, intended to depict the passions of Fear, Hate, Jealousy, and Love, both in tragedy and comedy, were destined for the stage, and the "Family Legend" was brought out in Edinburgh under Sir Walter's enthusiastic patronage and enjoyed a brilliant if brief success. In London also, another of Miss Baillie's plays, "De Montford," acted by Mrs. Siddons and Kemble, had a short run. It is, however, probable that her fame will depend chiefly on her lesser poems and songs, of which she has left some of great beauty. The purse is mentioned in two of Sir Walter's letters to the poetess in the following manner. Before receiving it Sir Walter writes :

"The promise of the purse has flattered my imagination so very agreeably that I cannot help sending you an ancient silver mouth-piece, to which, if it pleases your taste, you may adapt your intended labours ; this, besides, is a genteel way of tying you down to your promise : and to bribe you still further, I assure you it shall not be put to the purpose of holding bank-notes or vulgar bullion, but reserved as a place of deposit for some of my pretty little medals and nicknackatorics." And when the gift has duly been made and sent to him, he thus acknowledges it : " 1812. I ought not, even in modern gratitude, which may be moved by the gift of a purse, much less in minstrel sympathy, which values it more as your work than if it were stuffed with guineas, to have delayed thanking you, my kind friend, for such an elegant and acceptable token of your regard.

" My kindest and best thanks also attend the young lady who would not permit the purse to travel untenanted.[1] I have a great mind, before sealing this long scrawl, to send you a list of the contents of the purse as they at present stand.

" 1st. Miss Elizabeth Baillie's purse-penny, called by the learned a denarius of the Empress Faustina.

" 2nd. A gold brooch found in a bog in Ireland, which for aught I know fastened the mantle of an Irish princess in the days of Cathullia, or Neal of the Nine Hostages.

" 3rd. A toadstone [2]—a celebrated amulet which was never lent to any one unless upon a bond for a thousand marks for its being safely restored. It was sovereign for protecting new-born children and their mothers from the power of the fairies, and has been repeatedly borrowed from my mother on account of this virtue.

" 4th. A coin of Edward I. found in Dryburgh Abbey.

" 5th. A funeral ring with Dean Swift's hair,—so you see my nicknackatory is well supplied, though the purse is more valuable than all its contents."

[1] The purse contained an old coin from Joanna Baillie's niece, the daughter of the Doctor.

[2] See Plate XXI. for drawing of Amulet.

PLATE XV

" Hark the bagpipe's fitful wailing,
Not the pibroch loud and shrill,
But a dirge both low and solemn
Fit for ears of dying men
Marshalled for their latest battle
Never more to fight again."
*(Charles Edward at Versailles.—*AYTOUN.*)*

" Last noon beheld them full of lusty life
.   .   .   .   .   .
The earth is covered thick with other clay
Which her own clay shall cover heaped and pent ;
Rider and horse, friend, foe,—in one red burial blent."
(Childe Harold.)

SOLDIER'S MEMORANDUM BOOK FOUND ON THE FIELD OF WATERLOO

PIECE OF OAT-CAKE FOUND IN THE POCKET OF A DEAD HIGHLANDER ON THE FIELD OF CULLODEN

THESE pathetic records of two famous battlefields, while very different from each other, seem to be united by a common interest. Each bears witness to the fidelity, even to death, of its owner, and each reminds us of a fatal day in the annals of a great dynasty.

How the interesting little memorandum book came into Sir Walter's possession we learn by the following passage in *Paul's Letters* (p. 199). Speaking of the

smaller "reliques of the fray" which still strewed the field of battle he says:
"Among the last, those of most frequent occurrence were the military *livrets*, or
memorandum books of the French soldiers. I picked up one of these, which
shows by its order and arrangement the strict discipline which at one time was
maintained in the French army, when the soldier was obliged to enter in such an
accompt-book not only the state of his pay and equipments, but the occasions
on which he served and distinguished himself, and the punishments, if any,
which he had incurred. At the conclusion is a list of the duties of the private
soldier, amongst which is that of knowing how to dress his victuals and
particularly to make good soup. The *livret* in my possession appears to have
belonged to the Sieur Mallet, of the 2nd battalion of the 8th Regiment of the
Line; he had been in the service since the year 1791 until the 18th of June
1815, which day probably closed his account, and with it all his earthly hopes
and prospects."

Measurements of the Waterloo Book—4½ inches by 6¾ inches.

If the Sieur Mallet went forth to fight with all the "pomp and majesty of
war," our Scotch hero had to encounter not only the enemies of his Prince, but
another foe against whom no bravery will avail. How nearly absolute starvation was
the fate of Prince Charlie's followers the following account tells us, and the poor
little piece of oat-cake serves perhaps to illustrate the fact. "So scarce was food at
this critical juncture, that the Prince himself, on retiring to Culloden House, could
obtain no better refreshment than a little bread and whisky. He felt the utmost
anxiety regarding his men, among whom the pangs of hunger upon bodies exhausted
by fatigue must have been working effects most unpromising to his success; and
he gave orders, before seeking any repose, that the whole county should now be
mercilessly ransacked for the means of refreshment. His orders were not without
effect. Considerable supplies were procured, and subjected to the cooks' art at
Inverness, but the poor famished clansmen were destined never to taste these
provisions, the hour of battle arriving before they were prepared." [1]

The piece of oat-cake is made of coarsely ground oatmeal, and wrapped
carefully in a piece of paper, with the following words written on it—

"A piece of cake found in a Highlander's pocket on the field of Culloden the day
of the battle.   R. CHAMBERS."

[1] Chambers, *Hist. of Rebellion in Scotland, 1745, 1746,* vol. ii. pp. 81, 82.

PANEL FROM 'SPEAK A BIT'

PLATE XVI

ANCIENT BRONZE MASK

HE mask is 11 inches in length and 6½ broad, the horns being 18 inches in length. The ornament is in high relief, and very beautiful. This curious gabion was given to Sir Walter by Joseph Train. We are indebted to the Rev. Father Forbes Leith for the following interesting particulars regarding it.

"This mask is made of fine copper richly ornamented, and is constructed so as to cover the face of the wearer, having two long horns which bend backwards and downwards. The bronze measures 10½ inches in total length. It was found in a morass, on the farm of Torrs, in the parish of Kelton, Galloway, about the year 1820. It belongs in all probability to the later Celtic period of our history. It is probably not more ancient than the introduction of coinage into Britain, from 200 to 100 years B.C., and not much later than the close of the first century after Christ, when the Roman dominion in this country was firmly established.

"This peculiar bronze relic would appear to be almost unique in character. It was found in a district of Scotland where the Celtic element was largely developed among its inhabitants.

"It seems that it was intended to be used as part of some ornamental head-dress of a man. The heads of various animals, we know, have been used as decorations for head-pieces or helmets. The horns of cows as well as goats appear to have been worn by some of the Greeks."

A STEEL SKULL-CAP WITH GUARD OF VERY FINE CHAIN MAIL

The cap is 6¼ inches in diameter. Its history appears to be unknown. The mail guard, however, would seem to be similar to those described by Auguste Demmin in his *Weapons of War*. "The coat of mail (from the German *Kutte*), which preceded the armour composed of plates either of leather or steel, was called hauberk (from the German *Halsberge*, neck-protector). . . . The small hauberk was worn by all knights in the eighth century."

THE BRANKS

A facsimile model of the branks or bridle preserved in St. Mary's Church, St. Andrews.

This instrument, which is said to derive its name from the Gaelic *brangus*, an instrument for punishing petty offences, was formerly used for the correction of scolds in England and Scotland. In England it was often termed the "Scold's, or Gossip's, bridle," and appears to have taken the place of the ducking-stool. It is, however, said to be of Scotch origin, and was used in Scotland in the 16th century some fifty years before it appears to have been known in England. It is doubtful whether the branks was ever a legalised instrument of punishment, although corporations and lords of the manor in England, and town councils, kirk-sessions, and barony courts in Scotland, exercised the right of inflicting it. While men were put in the stocks or pillory, women wore the branks for such petty offences as are now termed breaches of the peace.

PLATE XVII

PRINCE CHARLIE'S QUAIGH

PRINCE CHARLIE'S quaigh is of oak, bound round by seven hoops, and mounted in plain bands of silver at top and bottom. It has the usual two small handles, but the bottom of the quaigh is of glass. On the upper rim of silver are the letters P. C. and on the lower is the following inscription : "This quaigh was presented in 1745 by Prince Charles to Campbell of Kinloch, one of his followers, whose widow gave it to Mrs. Stewart of Stenton, by whom it was gifted to Sir Walter Scott, Bart., in 1825." The quaigh measures 2 inches in height by 2 inches in diameter at the mouth, and $1\frac{3}{4}$ at the base. This quaigh was much valued by Sir Walter, and constantly used by him. "I should not omit, however," writes Mr. Lockhart, "that his Bordeaux was uniformly preceded by a small libation of his genuine mountain dew, which he poured with his own hand, *more majorum*, for each guest, making use for the purpose of such a multifarious collection of ancient Highland quaighs (little cups of curiously dovetailed wood inlaid with silver) as no lowland sideboard but his was ever equipped with, but commonly reserving for himself one that was peculiarly precious in his eyes, as having travelled from Edinburgh to Derby in the canteen of Prince Charlie. This relic had been presented to 'the wandering Ascanius' by some very careful followers, for its bottom is of glass, that he who quaffed might keep his eye the while upon the dirk hand of his companion." [1]

[1] *Life of Scott*, vol. v. pp. 339, 340.

BALFOUR OF BURLEIGH'S SNUFF-BOX

Balfour of Burleigh's snuff-box is an egg-shaped box of brass with delicately engraved ornament on it. It is much worn, and the ornamentation now almost undecipherable, but it seems to have consisted of foliage and figures. It is hinged at the end, the hinge being in high relief, with the lower half in the form of a crown— rather an inappropriate ornament for its owner! The length of the box is 3 inches, and the width 2 inches at the widest part.

It is unfortunately not known how this gabion came into Sir Walter's possession.

Balfour of Burleigh, immortalised by Sir Walter in *Old Mortality*, is described in the *Lives of Scottish Worthies* as a "little man, squint-eyed, and of a very fierce aspect. He was by some reckoned none of the most religious, yet he was always reckoned zealous and honest-hearted, courageous in every enterprise, and a brave soldier, seldom any escaping that came into his hands."[1]

In a note to *Old Mortality* Sir Walter tells us that the description of Burleigh's violent death in the novel is fictitious. He was wounded at Bothwell Bridge, and afterwards escaped to Holland. "His biographer seems simple enough to believe that he rose high in the Prince of Orange's favour," but having still a desire to be avenged upon the enemies of his cause in Scotland, he embarked for that country and died at sea. "It was reserved for this historian," continues Sir Walter, "to discover that the moderation of King William, and his prudent anxiety to prevent that perpetuating of factious quarrels which is called in modern times Reaction, were only adopted in consequence of the death of John Balfour called Burley."

NAPOLEON I.'s GOLD BEE-CLASPS

These clasps, composed of the well-known Napoleonic emblem, and which appear to be the clasps for a military cloak, were taken from Napoleon's carriage after the battle of Waterloo. The bees each measure $2\frac{1}{4}$ inches in length, the wings measure $1\frac{3}{8}$ across, the length of the whole clasp being six inches. Each bee has a stud underneath it to fasten it to the garment, and the clasp is formed by serpents in the form of an S, with an ornamental band round the centre.

[1] *Scottish Worthies*, Leith, 1816, p. 522.

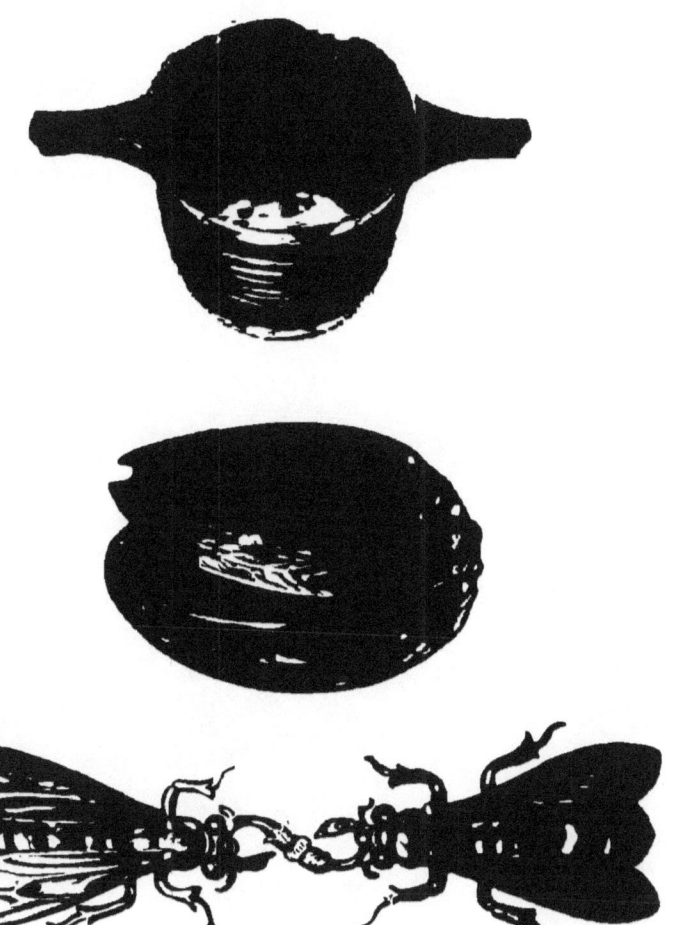

PANELS FROM 'SPEAK A BIT'

PLATE XVIII

BELT-PURSE OR SPORRAN IN STUDY

THIS purse, of which, unfortunately, we possess no history, is of red plush with a red woollen binding, and lined with pale red leather. It has two divisions with a small drawing-up bag fastened against the central piece of leather. The clasp is semicircular with an upright grooved pin and movable ring, with which it could be fastened to the belt. It is of brass and perfectly plain. The size of the purse is $7\frac{1}{2}$ inches in length by 5 inches at hinge of clasp.

POCKET-BOOK WORKED BY FLORA MACDONALD

"Give me back my trusty comrades,
Give me back my Highland Maid,
Nowhere beats the heart so kindly,
As beneath the tartan plaid."
(*Charles Edward at Versailles.*—AYTOUN.)

The pocket-book, which when shut measures $4\frac{1}{2}$ by 6 inches, is embroidered with wool on canvas, and bound with faded ribbons. It is lined with rose-pink sarcenet, and most likely the ribbon was of the same colour. It has four pockets for letters, very ingeniously contrived, and fastened together with a rounded flap, tied by a thin purplish-coloured ribbon. The book is embroidered in a zigzag pattern, in various colours. A letter relating to the history of this precious gabion is preserved in one of the pockets, from which we give the following extracts.

LEITH, *6th May* 1825.

SIR·WALTER SCOTT, BART.

SIR,

. . . This letter is accompanied by a curiosity of no ordinary interest, a pocket-book wrought by the hands of the celebrated Flora Macdonald, and of which, sir, I now most respectfully solicit your acceptance. I need not mention the motives which have induced me to do myself the honour, and to place in your hands this little relic—it is enough to say that it has been given to Sir Walter Scott. In order to do away, as far as I possibly can, any idea of imposition which might intrude, I shall state to you how it came into my possession. In the summer of 1809 my father, Duncan Campbell, the Supervisor of Excise in Glasgow, was appointed by the Board to accompany one Collector Malcolm in surveying all the salt stocks on the west and north coast of Scotland and the Isles. In the excursion my mother and myself accompanied him. Amongst other places at which the vessel (a Revenue Cruiser) touched was Port Ree in the Isle of Skye. During our stay in that harbour we visited a Mr. Macdonald of Kingsburgh, where we met with a sister of the Attic heroine, an elderly widow lady. My mother being of the same name, and a native of the North Highlands, an intimacy very soon took place, and the gift of the pocket-book was the result. I am sorry to add that a lock of Prince Charlie's hair, which the book contained at the time it was given, has been lost. The letters M. M., which you will observe on the outside, are thus explained. Flora, it would appear, had intended the pocket-book as a present to a Mr. Martin Martin—at that time a clergyman in the Island,—but he having died, it never reached its destination.

I am, SIR,

With the most profound respect,

Your obedient servant,

ALEX. CAMPBELL.

No words of ours are needed to enhance the fame of Flora Macdonald, nor would it be possible to enter here into the details of her heroic undertaking; but we cannot refrain from recalling the interesting description of this famous person contained in Boswell's *Tour of the Hebrides*. He and Dr. Johnson arrived at

Kingsburgh on 12th September 1773, where they were hospitably received by Mr. Macdonald. Boswell thus continues : " There was a comfortable parlour with a good fire, and a dram went round. By and by supper was served, at which there appeared the lady of the house, the celebrated Miss Flora Macdonald. She is a little woman, of a genteel appearance, and uncommonly mild and well-bred. To see Dr. Samuel Johnson, the great champion of the English Tories, salute Miss Flora Macdonald in the Isle of Sky, was a striking sight, for, though somewhat congenial in their notions, it was very improbable they should meet here.

.   .   .   .

"The room where we lay was a celebrated one. Dr. Johnson's bed was the very bed in which the grandson of the unfortunate King James II. lay, on one of the nights after the failure of his rash attempt in 1745-46, while he was eluding the pursuit of the emissaries of Government, which had offered thirty thousand pounds as a reward for apprehending him. To see Dr. Samuel Johnson lying in that bed, in the Isle of Sky, in the house of Miss Flora Macdonald, struck me with such a groupe of ideas as it is not easy for words to describe, as they passed through the mind. He smiled and said, ' I have no ambitious thoughts in it.' "

Who would not wish to have been present the following morning after breakfast when Dr. Johnson "spoke of Prince Charles being there, and asked Mrs. Macdonald ' *Who* was with him ? We are told, Madam, in England, there was one Miss Flora Macdonald with him.' " She said, "they were very right," and perceiving Dr. Johnson's curiosity, though he had delicacy enough not to question her, very obligingly entertained him with a recital of the particulars which she herself knew of that escape, which does so much honour to the humanity, fidelity, and generosity of the Highlanders. Dr. Johnson listened to her with placid attention and said, "All this should be written down."

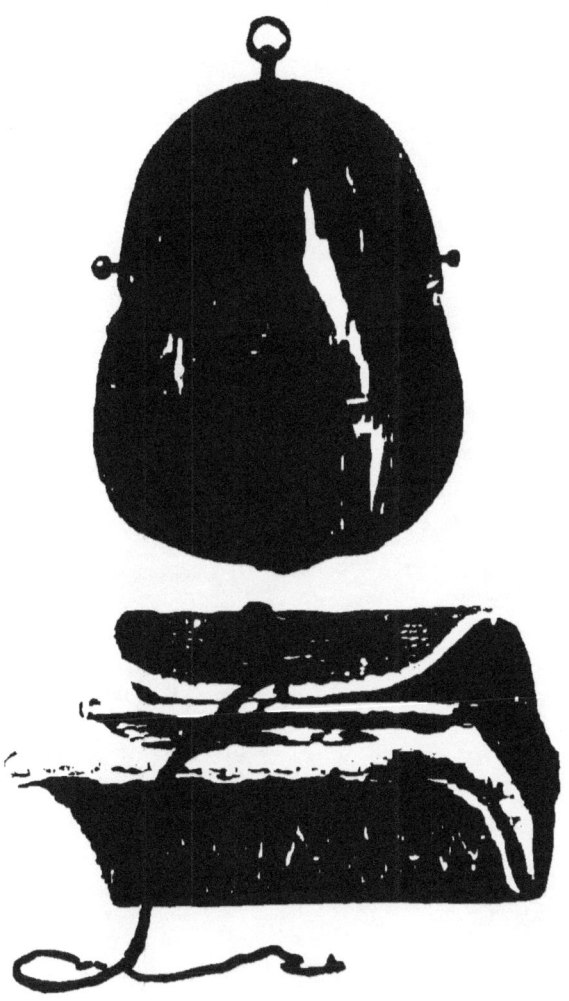

PLATE XIX

ROB ROY'S GUN AND SWORD

"And thus among the rocks he lived,
Through summer's heat and winter's snow:
The eagle he was lord above,
And Rob was lord below."—WORDSWORTH.

ROB ROY'S gun is an old flint-lock gun with long barrel, inlaid with three silver bands and silver plate bearing initials R. M. C. (for Robert Macgregor Campbell).[1] This is the same gun with which his son, Robin Oig, shot M'Laren of Invernenty. The barrel is octagonal. The stock has a brass plate with an engraved design and another on the top with a shell pattern. The trigger guard is also of brass. The barrel is 4 feet in length, and the stock 17 inches.

Rob Roy's sword is a fine "old Highland Broadsword, with Andrea Ferrara blade and basket hilt." It is 37 inches in length, the blade being $32\frac{1}{2}$ by $1\frac{1}{2}$ inches. Enlargements of hilt and stock drawn half real size.

On each side the blade has the name Andrea Ferrara with three orbs and crosses. The hilt is of scroll work with flat plates perforated with round and heart-shaped holes. The grip is covered with spirally carved wood, and the pommel is a flattened knob ornamented with dots and lines.

[1] Introduction to *Rob Roy*, Cent. Ed., p. 39.

Rob Roy's name is so familiar as a hero of romance, and the real facts of his history are so intermingled with those of a legendary nature, that it is perhaps difficult to disentangle the two, and to picture to ourselves the man as he really appeared to his contemporaries. Robert Macgregor, commonly styled Rob Roy, was the younger son of Donald Macgregor of Glengyle. His mother was a Campbell of Glenfalloch, and Robert afterwards adopted her name when his own had been abolished by Act of Parliament. Robert's own designation was of Inversnaid, but later in life he also acquired some kind of right to the property of Craig Royston, lying on the east side of Loch Lomond. To this, possibly, as well as to his colouring, he owed his sobriquet of Rob Roy. The exact date of his birth, and even of his death, is uncertain ; but it is probable that he was born about the middle of the seven-teenth century, as he is said to have died about 1733, an aged man. To follow Robert through his chequered career from his first reputed appearance among the scenes of war and plunder following the Revolution, through his more peaceful days of cattle-dealing, ending in the wild days of his "cateran" life and political enter-prise, would be too long a task, but the following descriptions taken from Sir Walter's historical introduction to the novel of *Rob Roy*, may help us to form a just idea of this remarkable personage :—

"His stature was not of the tallest, but his person was uncommonly strong and compact. The greatest peculiarities of his frame were the breadth of his shoulders, and the great and almost disproportionate length of his arms—so remarkable indeed that it was said he could, without stooping, tie the garters of his Highland hose, which are placed two inches below the knee. His countenance was open, manly, stern at periods of danger, but frank and cheerful in his hours of festivity. His hair was dark red, thick and frizzled, and curled short round the face. His fashion of dress showed, of course, the knees and upper part of the leg, which was described to' me as resembling that of a Highland bull, hirsute with red hair, and evincing muscular strength similar to that animal. To these personal qualifications must be added a masterly use of the Highland sword, in which his length of arm gave him great advantage, and a perfect and intimate knowledge of all the recesses of the wild country in which he harboured, and the character of the various individuals, whether friends or hostile, with whom he might come in contact. His mental qualities seem to have been less adapted to the circumstances in which he was placed. Though the descendant of the bloodthirsty Ciar Mhor, he inherited none of his ancestor's ferocity. On the contrary, Rob Roy avoided every appearance of cruelty, and it is not averred that he was ever the means of unnecessary bloodshed, or the actor in any deed which could lead the way to it. His schemes of plunder were contrived and executed with equal boldness and sagacity, and were almost universally successful, from the skill with which they were laid, and the secrecy and rapidity with which they were executed. Like Robin Hood of England he was a kind and gentle robber, and, while he took from the rich, was liberal in relieving the poor. This might in part be policy; but the universal tradition of the country speaks it to have arisen from a better motive.

"All whom I have conversed with, and I have in my youth seen some who knew Rob Roy personally, give him the character of a benevolent and humane man 'in his way.'

"This singular man died in bed in his own house in the parish of Balquhidder. He was buried in the churchyard of the same parish, where his tombstone is only distinguished by a rude attempt at the figure of a broadsword."[1]

[1] Introduction to *Rob Roy*, Centenary Edition, pp. 17 and 18.

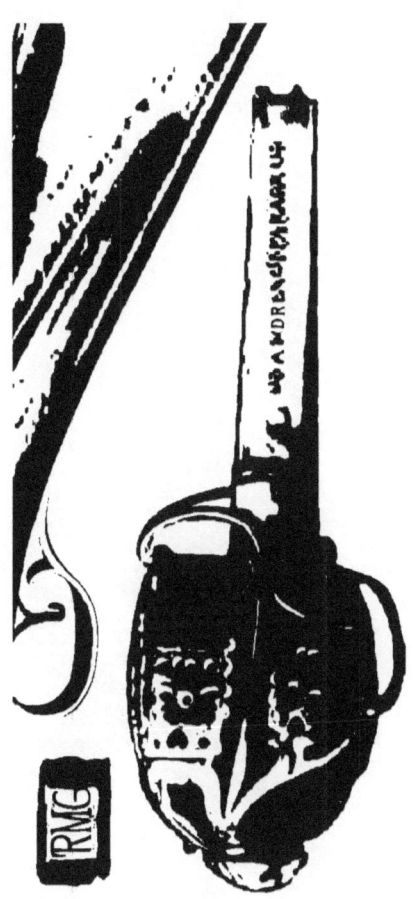

PANELS FROM ERSKINE'S PULPIT

PLATE XX

TWO PAIRS OF THUMBSCREWS OR THUMBIKINS

HIS cruel little instrument of torture was introduced into practice by the Scottish Privy Council in the 17th century. As shown by the examples here given, the thumbscrews varied slightly in form; but we should fear their variations made little difference to the victims "whose thumbs could be broken or hopelessly destroyed by the screw." [1]

The well-known Mr. William Carstares was, for complicity in some of the plots of the day, tortured by the thumbscrews for fully an hour. After the Revolution he became Principal of the University of Edinburgh and confidential adviser to William III. regarding the affairs of Scotland. The identical thumbscrews by which he had suffered were presented to him by the Privy Council, and were long preserved in the family. The following anecdote in connection with the instrument was handed down by his descendants. " I have heard, Principal," said King William to him, " that you were tortured with something they call thumbikins; pray what sort of instrument of torture is it?" " I will show it you," answered Carstares, "the next time I have the honour to wait upon your Majesty." Soon after, accordingly, the Principal brought the thumbikins to be shown to the King. "I must put in my thumbs here; now Principal, turn the screw. Oh not so gently; another turn—another. Stop, stop! No more! Another turn, I am afraid, would make me confess anything." [2]

[1] *Scottish National Memorials.*
[2] R. Chambers, *Domestic Annals of Scotland.*

The following letter, endorsed by Sir Walter—"Mr. Alexander, with a pair of Thumbscrews," accompanied one of the instruments (the one to the left) here portrayed, and gives a vivid picture of the times when such cruelties were practised by law.

6 GEORGE STREET,
21st May 1819.

SIR,

   At Jedburgh, during last Spring Circuit, I met with Mr. J. Richardson, whom one evening, as he was describing some Memorials of Ancient Times which he had seen at Abbotsford, I asked if there was among them anything like the thumbikins so well known at one period in Scotland. I told him I was in possession of a pair; that I had often wished to give them to Mr. Scott, but had felt a delicacy in doing so. Richardson said he should mention to you what I told him; and yesterday I learned that you would be happy to accept them. Of these thumbikins I can give no satisfactory account. My mother's family has, for time immemorial, resided in Ayrshire. During the persecution under Charles II. her great grandfather, Hugh Miller, or some still more distant progenitor of that name, underwent considerable hardships. He was long a prisoner in Ayr Jail, and more than once it is reported suffered torture. The jailer's daughter was young, lovely, and tender-hearted, and taking compassion on Hugh's desolate condition, her kindness, which commenced by feeding him through a wicket with bread, unknown to her father, at last terminated in a devoted attachment and love which was strongly and honourably felt on the part of the hardy prisoner. After about two years' confinement he was somehow liberated. He soon after married her, and here am I, a direct descendant from this philanthropic fair one and this sturdy Covenanter. My testimony to these facts is oral and traditionary, yet from my knowledge of the habits of my forefathers I have entire confidence in what they have thus related. That Hugh suffered by means of thumbikins, or that these are the identical instruments, I must not say; yet such is the report, and these thumbikins have been long at least in my mother's family. But be that as it may, thumbikins they certainly are—old, stern, and angry-like; and where inquiry would now be vain I have just allowed myself to believe them the very instruments which screwed the thumbs of hardy Hugh, and wrung the heart of tender Mary.

Thus descended of firm and faithful Covenanters, educated in their strictest tenets, taught to revere their memory and their doings, and even inclined to glory in their efforts, which I believed were often prompted and guided by fanaticism, am I false to the memory of my ancestors in thus parting with what most powerfully serves to suggest their sufferings and their constancy? Certainly I am not. I have long thought, perhaps with childish solicitude, regarding such a trifling relic, how I might without impertinence resign it to its best and most legitimate custodier; and in proportion as my fancy and my veneration was alive to all associated with this relic, have felt the higher wish to put it into the keeping of one whom I deem the truest representative of all that is national. In short, I wished it in your possession, and am proud to know you will accept it.

Accept then this trifling memorial of earlier times, as a testimony of my high esteem for your character, and admiration of your genius, and you will kindly oblige,

SIR,

Your very humble Servant,

GABRIEL ALEXANDER.

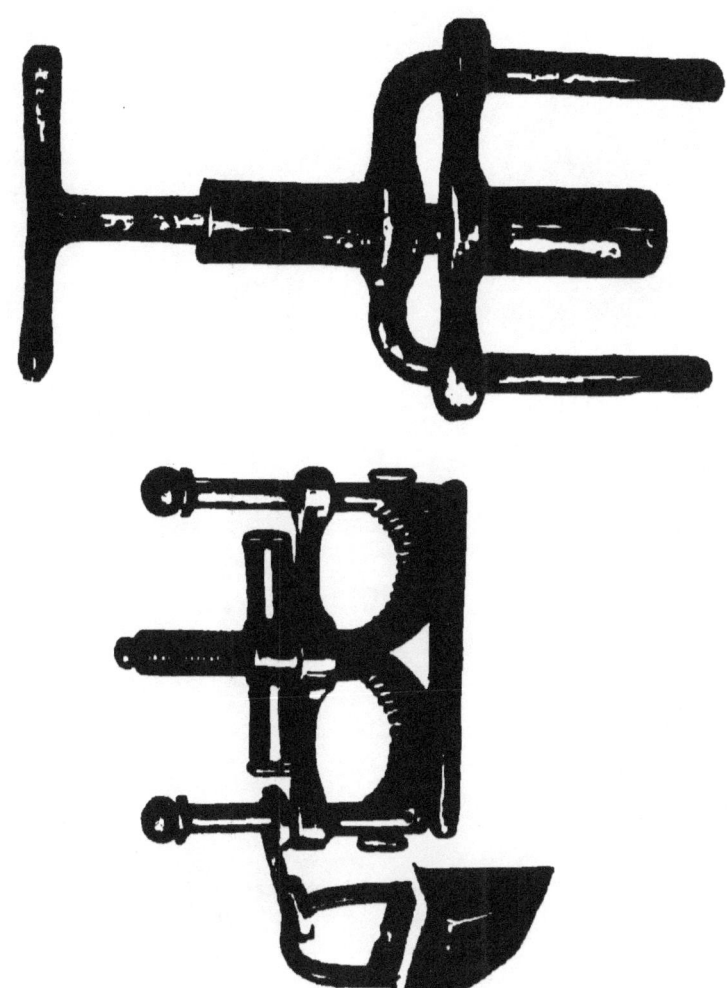

PANELS FROM 'SPEAK A BIT'

PLATE XXI

ROB ROY'S PURSE

HE purse is 4½ inches broad by 4 inches deep, and is made of brown leather, much worn. It has two divisions, and has evidently been sewn to a belt,—the holes of the stitches being visible in four places at the back. The front of the purse is gathered together in two folds by a leather thong, and the flap is fastened with a button. It contains a card with the following lines: " This purse, with a dirk now (1818) in the possession of Mr. Young, Castle Douglas, was given by Rob Roy to Maxwell, Esq., of Straquhan in the parish of Dunscore. After this gentleman was drowned in the River Fleet, the purse and dirk became the property of Thos. Walker, an old servant, whose son, through the intermedium of a friend, gave this purse to Joseph Train, who takes the liberty of presenting it to Walter Scott, Esq."

In the Abbotsford MSS. we find the following note which completes this account.

" The generous supervisor, Mr. Train, visited Sir Walter in Edinburgh in May 1816, a few days after the publication of the *Antiquary*, carrying with him several relics which he wished to present to his collection, among others *a Purse that had belonged to Rob Roy.*"

HELEN MACGREGOR'S BROOCH

The brooch is of silver, circular in form, and of the style generally termed Celtic. It is a six-pointed star with a thistle and two leaves between, and alternating with each point. The drawing is full size. The brooch appears to have been the chief ornament in the dress of the Gael, both in Ireland and Scotland, and was used by the women to fasten the plaid and other portions of their attire, from which Pinkerton thinks may be derived the usual perquisite of women, *pin-money*.

Although a woman of "fierce and haughty temper," this high-spirited chieftainess must have possessed warm feelings and no mean taste for music, as evinced by *Rob Roy's Lament*, a fine piece of pipe music composed by her to express her grief when she and her husband were forced to leave the banks of Loch Lomond, about the year 1712. To compensate for our meagre knowledge of Helen we venture to quote Francis Osbaldistone's description of her in the novel of *Rob Roy*, not omitting the worthy Bailie's comment on her appearance.

"I have seldom seen a finer or more commanding form than this woman. She might be between the term of forty and fifty years, and had a countenance which must once have been of a masculine cast of beauty, though now imprinted with deep lines by exposure to rough weather, and perhaps by the wasting influence of grief and passion, its features were only strong, harsh, and expressive. She wore her plaid, not drawn around her head and shoulders as is the fashion of the women in Scotland, but disposed around her body, as the Highland soldiers wear theirs. She had a man's bonnet, with a feather in it, an unsheathed sword in her hand, and a pair of pistols at her girdle.

"'It's Helen Campbell, Rob's wife,' said the Bailie, in a whisper of considerable alarm; 'and there will be broken heads amang us or it's lang.'"[1]

TOADSTONE AMULET

The amulet, in length 2 inches, and in breadth $1\frac{3}{4}$, is a flat, heart-shaped stone of a dark reddish brown, veined with shades of lighter colour. It is surrounded by a silver mounting in the form of leaves, tied down by a double chain. An oval ring is fixed at the top, to allow of it being worn on a ribbon or chain,—a use to which it seems often to have been put, as Sir Walter tells us in the following description of this gabion: "A toadstone, a celebrated amulet, which was never lent to any one unless upon a bond for a thousand marks for its being safely restored. It was sovereign for protecting new-born children and their mothers from the power of the fairies, and has been repeatedly borrowed from my mother on account of this virtue."[2]

[1] *Rob Roy*, Centenary Edition, p. 342.   [2] Abbotsford MSS.

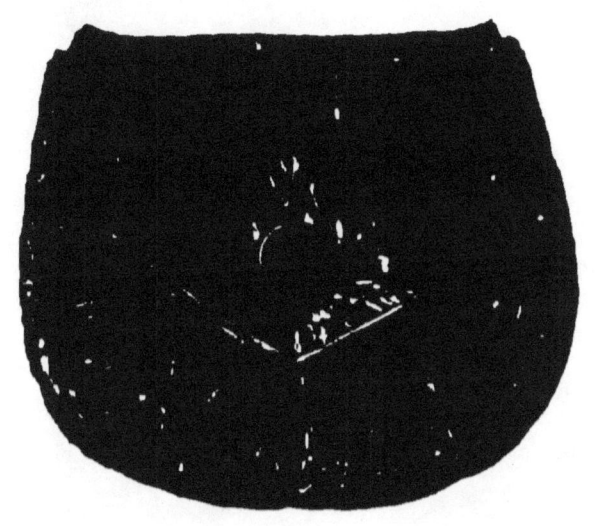

PLATE XXII

BORDER WAR-HORN

THIS horn was a trophy of one of Sir Walter's "raids" into Liddesdale. For seven successive years he made these expeditions, accompanied by his excellent friend, Mr. Shortreed, Sheriff-Substitute for Roxburghshire. The charming descriptions of "Charlie's Hope" and its inhabitants, and much of the material for the *Minstrelsy of the Scottish Border*, owe their origin to these journeys; and though we do not know how early Sir Walter had any definite object in his researches, he was, as Mr. Shortreed expressed it, "makin' himself a' the time." This good friend also thus graphically describes the acquisition of the war-horn.

"It was that same season, I think," says Mr. Shortreed, "that Sir Walter got from Dr. Elliot the large old border war-horn which ye may still see hanging in the armoury at Abbotsford. How *great* he was when he was made master o' *that!* I believe it had been found in Hermitage Castle, and one of the doctor's servants had used it many a day as a grease-horn for his scythe before they discovered its history. When cleaned out it was never a hair the worse—the original chain, hoop, and mouthpiece of steel were all entire, just as you now see them. Sir Walter carried it home all the way from Liddesdale to Jedburgh, slung about his neck like Johnny Gilpin's bottle, while I was intrusted with an ancient bridlebit, which we had likewise picked up.

> 'The feint o' pride—na pride had he . . .
> A lang kail-gully hung down by his side,
> And a great mickle nowt-horn to rout on had he.'

8

And meikle and sair we routed on't, and 'hotched and blew, wi' micht and main.'
Oh what pleasant days! And then a' the nonsense had cost us naething. We never
put hand in pocket for a week on end. Toll-bars there were none—and indeed I
think our haill charges were a feed o' corn to our horses in the gangin' and comin' at
Riccarton mill."

The war-horn, which resembles an ordinary cow horn, is hooped with iron. It
has a double chain attached to each end by rings. The length of the horn is 22½
inches, the diameter nearly 4 inches.

JAMES VI.'s HUNTING-BOTTLE

The hunting-bottle is contained in an old tooled and gilt leather case, which
has a brass lock and catch highly ornamented with leaf and floral design. The
bottle is oval with glass stopper.

The size is 8 inches by 4½.

This bottle was presented to Sir Walter by his friend and valued amanuensis,
Mr. Huntly Gordon, the son of Major Pryse Gordon, Sir Walter's cicerone on the
field of Waterloo in 1815.

Sir Walter, in a note to the *Fortunes of Nigel*, alludes to the hunting-bottle as
follows : "The author, among other nicknacks of antiquity, possesses a leathern flask
like those carried by sportsmen, which is labelled 'King James's Hunting-Bottle.'"
Unfortunately, he adds, "with what authority is uncertain."

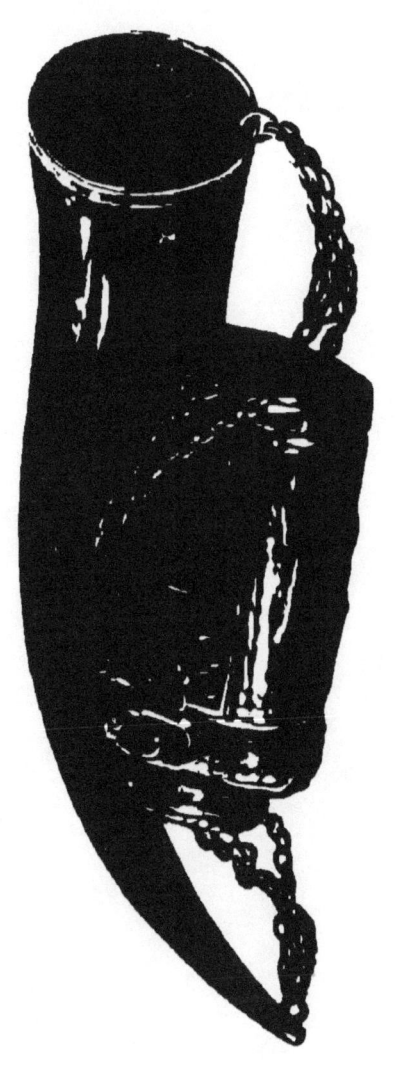

PLATE XXIII

A POLYGAR'S KNIFE

 WEAPON with a broad curved blade. The blade damascened with gold in cuneiform and line designs. The handle is mounted with brass and ornamented with quatrefoil and crescents in high relief, and enriched by 26 small rubies.

Length 25 inches.

A PERSIAN DAGGER AND SHEATH

This dagger is 14 inches in length. The sheath is of wood covered with red velvet. The hilt is of iron, beautifully damascened in gold, in flowers and leaves. The blade is slightly fluted. The mounting of the sheath is also beautifully engraved.

A MALAY KRIS

With grotesque ivory handle in the form of a bird. The blade waved and fluted.

Length 18 inches.

CASE OF HUNTING-KNIVES, OR COUTEAUX DE CHASSE

This case of hunting-knives, called also a "Slashing Hanger," is said to have belonged to Prince Charlie, which its apparent date and French origin may corroborate.

The hilts and sheath are ornamented with chased ormolu mounts of the time of Louis XIV. The handle of the large knife bears a figure of Diana. The case also contains three small knives, a two-pronged fork, and a pointed instrument with a perforated hole like the eye of a large needle. The case is $20\frac{1}{2}$ inches long, by $3\frac{3}{4}$ inches at its broadest part.

ROB ROY'S DIRK

"A very long old Highland dirk, with Andrea Ferrara double channelled blade, formerly belonged to Rob Roy."[1] It is $24\frac{1}{2}$ inches long. The blade is 20 inches, with a carved interlaced handle finished on the top with a flat circular plate of silver, and a knob. The sheath is black leather, mounted with four bands of silver, two of which head pockets containing a knife and a two-pronged fork. Both handles are carved with interlaced work. The sheath has a plain silver ring at upper end.

This dirk is, we may hope, the same which is connected with a dramatic scene at the close of Rob Roy's life, given as follows in the historical preface to the novel. "There is a tradition . . . that while on his deathbed he (Rob Roy) learned that a member of a family with whom he was at enmity proposed to visit him. 'Raise me from my bed,' said the invalid, 'throw my plaid around me, and bring me my claymore, dirk, and pistols—it shall never be said that a foeman saw Rob MacGregor defenceless and unarmed.' "

A TARTAR SWORD IN BRASS-MOUNTED SHAGREEN SCABBARD

The slightly convex grip is of fluted ebony, mounted in brass and engraved in floral and foliated patterns with ground in small raised dots. The sheath is of wood covered with shagreen and ornamented by three raised oval medallions in brass, with the same floral patterns and dotted ground throughout. Length 23 inches.

[1] *Abbotsford Catalogue*, p. 22.

PLATE XXIV

ROB ROY'S SPORRAN[1] AND SKENE DHU

ROB ROY'S sporran is of very strong thick skin with a semicircular clasp, ornamented with concentric circles, and a single line with fine dog-tooth on the upper side. The skin is sewn to the clasp by thongs, and the front has a raised five-pointed star, and a waving line. The top of the clasp is ornamented with lines, and has had three knobs. At the back is a brass knob in the centre, and on either side a strong flat metal loop. This gabion was given to Sir Walter by Mr. Constable, as we learn by the following letter :—

MR. SCOTT TO MR. CONSTABLE.

"ABBOTSFORD, 11*th October* 1817.

"DEAR SIR,—I have to return you my best thanks for the curious letters—one by my father's grandfather, the Laird of Newmains; one respecting Harden, who appears to have been, like some of his descendants, occasionally short of cash. They are, however, a thriving generation in their way, and taking them on the whole. I have bought Totfield, which will clear the *sporran* which you have so lately filled. I fancy, by the very curious purse you have so obligingly given me, you had a mind to give me a hint how to keep my cash: for if I once could put it into Rob Roy's leathern convenience, I defy any one to find the means of getting it out again. Hitherto our united ingenuity has not been able to find the mode of opening it. However, if I can put no money into the

---

[1] The sporran has, we believe, never been opened.'

Highlandman's sporran I can contrive to make them put some into mine, which
is as much to the purpose.   (Signed) WALTER SCOTT.

"The stone from Linlithgow is very curious."

It is doubtful whether we may assert this sporran to be the same as that
described at page 392 of the novel of *Rob Roy*, but we cannot refrain from quoting
the passage so appropriate to this gabion.

"'I advise no man to attempt opening this sporran till he has my secret,' said
Rob Roy, and then twisting one button in one direction, and another in another,
pulling one stud upward, and pressing another downward, the mouth of the purse,
which was bound with massive silver-plate, opened and gave admittance to his hand.
He made me remark that a small steel pistol was concealed within the purse, the
trigger of which was connected with the mounting and made part of the machinery,
so that the weapon could be discharged, and in all probability its contents lodged in
the person of any one who, being unacquainted with the secret, should tamper with the
lock which secured his treasure. 'This,' said he, touching the pistol, 'this is the
keeper of my privy purse.'"

Size—$8\frac{1}{4}$ in. long, by $5\frac{1}{4}$ in. at the hinges of clasp, and $6\frac{1}{4}$ in. at the broadest part
of the bag.

Rob Roy's skene dhu is a strong dangerous-looking weapon, 8 in. in length,
including handle, and $1\frac{3}{8}$ in. at widest part of blade. The handle is cross hatched by
deep cut lines and mounted with silver. The end is set with a pale-coloured cairn-
gorm which is drawn full size. The blade has the maker's name, M'Leod, engraved
upon it. The sheath is of black leather, mounted at both ends with broad bands of
silver.

The skene dhu, or black knife, which formed part of a Highlander's equipment,
was used for the purpose of despatching game, or for other servile purposes for which
they objected to use their dirks. Unfortunately nothing is known of the history of
this weapon, nor is it known how it came into Sir Walter's possession.

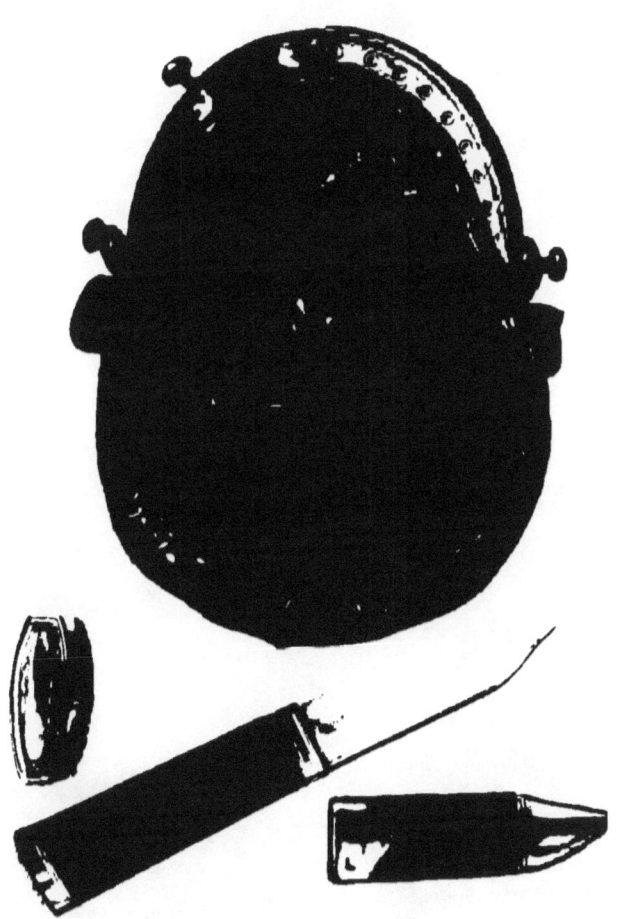

PLATE XXV

THE DOOR OF "THE HEART OF MIDLOTHIAN"—
THE OLD TOLBOOTH OF EDINBURGH—
AND ITS KEYS

THIS door, which is built into the west end of the house, was presented to Sir Walter by the Magistrates of Edinburgh in 1817, when the ancient prison of Edinburgh was pulled down. In the previous year Sir Walter, in a letter to Mr. Terry, thus alludes to this interesting addition to his "gabions."

"I expect to get some decorations from the old Tolbooth of Edinburgh, particularly the cope stones of the doorway, or lintels, as we call them, and a niche or two, one very handsome indeed! Better get a niche *from* the Tolbooth than a niche *in* it, to which such building-operations are apt to bring the projectors."

The Tolbooth, so intimately connected not only with the long history of national crime and misery, but with brighter days of loyal parliaments, and ennobled by the names of some of those who were imprisoned within its walls, appears to have been in part of great antiquity, as it was already old and ruinous in the reign of Queen Mary, and its destruction was even then contemplated. The Tolbooth stood close to the Church of St. Giles, occupying

half the width of the High Street. "Antique in form, gloomy and haggard
in aspect, its black stanchioned windows opening through its dingy walls
like the apertures of a hearse, it was calculated to impress all beholders with
a due and deep sense of what was meant in Scottish law by *squalor carceris*."[1]

It was composed of two parts, one more ancient and solid than the other,
and much resembling a border tower,—it had indeed probably been a kind of
peel, or house of defence, used for public purposes by the citizens of Edinburgh.—
It may very likely have been the very "pretorium burgi de Edinburgi " in which
a parliament was held in 1438, to deliberate on the measures necessitated by
the murder of James I.   Here Queen Mary assembled her parliaments, and
here, *on the door of the Tolbooth*, the citizens of Edinburgh by night fixed libels
charging the Earl of Bothwell with the murder of Darnley, and doubtless other
documents of the same nature at divers times.   The chief entrance to the prison,
and the only one used in later times, was at the bottom of the turret next St.
Giles's Church.   *The gateway was of carved stone, and the door of ponderous
massiveness and strength, having besides the lock a flap-padlock.*

The first floor of the prison was occupied by the hall, originally used as
Parliament House, and in which in later days a curious double window was
pointed out as having then formed the door through which the sovereign
entered.   It is said that on these occasions a sort of temporary bridge was thrown
between this aperture and a house on the other side of the street, by which
the sovereign in regal robes made his state entry.

In more modern times one end of the hall was partitioned into two small
rooms for the use of the chaplain of the prison.   At the end of the apartment
hung a board on which were inscribed the following verses :

> " A Prison is a house of care,
>   A place where none can thrive,
>   A touchstone true to try a friend,
>   A grave for men alive.
>
> Sometimes a place of right,
>   Sometimes a place of wrong,
> Sometimes a place for jades and thieves,
>   And honest men among."

---

[1] Chambers, *Traditions of Edinburgh.*

Of the *honest men* imprisoned in the Tolbooth, one great name stands foremost. Here Montrose spent his last days, and from here

> " Came the hero from his prison,
> To the scaffold and the doom."

After the execution the head was "set on the Tolbooth of Edinburgh," and so fearful were his enemies of its being removed that "there was a new cross prick appointed of iron to cross the former prick, whereon his head was fixed, which was speedily done that his head should not be removed."[1]   How Montrose had viewed the fate reserved for him we learn by his gallant words to the magistrates of Edinburgh, who visited him in his prison the day before his death. "I am much beholden to the Parliament," he said, "for the great honour they have decreed me.   I am prouder to have had my head fixed upon the top of the prison in view of the present and succeeding ages than if they had decreed me a golden statue in the market-place, or that my picture should be hung in the king's bedchamber.   I am thankful for that effectual method of preserving the memory of my devotion to my beloved sovereign."[2]

Less than a hundred years later the Tolbooth became the scene of the famous Porteous Riot.   From the vivid description given of this tragic event by Sir Walter in *The Heart of Midlothian* we choose the following extracts, as they bear more particularly on the subject we are considering.

When the mob had surrounded the prison, "a select body of the rioters thundered at the door of the jail and demanded instant admission.   No one answered, for the outer keeper had prudently made his escape with the keys at the commencement of the riot, and was nowhere to be found.   The door was instantly

---

[1] Nichol's *Diary*.

[2] "A rare work printed in 1676, and entitled Binning's *Light to the Art of Gunnery*, contains a curious story regarding the head of Montrose. 'In the year 1650,' says Binning, 'I was in the Castle of Edinburgh. One remarkable instance I had in shooting at that mirror of his time for loyalty and gallantry, James Marquis of Montrose his head, standing on the pinnacle of the Tolbooth of Edinburgh : but that Providence had ordered that head to be taken down with more honour.   I admired of its abiding, for the ball took the stone joining the stone whereon it stood, which stone fell down and killed a drummer and a soldier or two, on their march between the Luckenbooths and the Church, and the head remained till by his Majesty it was ordered to be taken down and buried with such honour as was due to it.' Very shortly after the ' True Funerals ' of Montrose, the head of his great enemy Argyll replaced his on the Tolbooth." *Montrose and the Covenanters,* Napier.

assailed with sledge-hammers, iron-crows, and the coulters of ploughs ready provided for the purpose, with which they prised, heaved, and battered for some time with little effect—the door being of double oak planks, clenched, both end-long and athwart, with broad-headed nails, and so hung and secured as to yield to no means of forcing without the expenditure of much time." . . . "The passive resistance of the Tolbooth" continued to baffle the conspirators until at "length a voice was heard tó pronounce the words 'Try it with fire.' The rioters, with a unanimous shout, called for combustibles; and as all their wishes seemed to be instantly supplied, they were soon in possession of two or three empty tar-barrels. A huge, red, glaring bonfire soon arose close to the door of the prison, sending up a tall column of smoke and flames against its antique turrets and strongly grated windows, and illuminating the ferocious faces and wild gestures of the rioters who surrounded the place, as well as the pale and anxious groups of those who from windows in the vicinage watched the progress of this alarming scene. The mob fed the fire with whatever they could find fit for the purpose. The flames roared and crackled among the heaps of nourishment piled on the fire, and a terrible shout soon announced that the door had kindled, and was in the act of being destroyed. The fire was suffered to decay, but long ere it was quite extinguished the most forward of the rioters rushed, in their impatience, one after another, over its smouldering remains."

This episode seems to have been the last of any public interest connected with the Tolbooth, and before another century had elapsed the building had disappeared, leaving only the memory of the crimes and sorrows of which it had been the silent witness.